DONKEY RESCUE

DONKEY RESCUE

Pamela Cockerill

CANONGATE · KELPIES

First published in 1990
by Canongate Kelpies
Reprinted 1994

British Library Cataloguing-in-Publication Data
Cockerill, Pamela
Donkey Rescue.
I. Title
823.914 [J]

ISBN 0 86241 317 6

Printed and bound in Denmark by Nørhaven A/S

CANONGATE PRESS, 14 FREDERICK STREET,
EDINBURGH EH2 2HB

For my family, without whose presence this book would have been finished much sooner.

CONTENTS

You Can't Hide a Donkey

'D'you mean they're going to kill him, just to make money?' the girl asked.

Terry flinched and took a step backwards, pushing his heavy glasses back up his nose. Her voice was quiet but her green eyes glinted angrily.

'Looks like it,' he mumbled. He knew her name was Fiona, but he had never spoken to her before, although she had been in his class a whole term. She had joined his local Comprehensive in May. He had felt sorry for her, starting a new school when everyone else had got their friends sorted out. He hated new scenes himself. But she had seemed quite self-contained and indifferent, and he wouldn't have spoken to her now if she hadn't come up to him as he stood by the crumbling sea-wall, staring miserably at the ebbing tide. The sea looked cold and grey, although it was July.

'Well. What have you done about it so far?'

'I spoke to the owner, Mr Fells. He said Zebedee was very old — twenty-three he said — and he'd come to the end of his life anyway. Mr Fells is quite nice actually.' He added apologetically, 'After all it's not as if it's any of my business, like my Dad says.'

'He can afford to be nice if he's planning on getting thousands of pounds for the field. And murder is everybody's business.' She hopped over the low wall and a cold sea-wind lifted her straggling red hair and wrapped it around her thin neck. It was the reddest hair and the thinnest neck he had ever seen.

'Come on,' she said, and crunched across the shingle without waiting to see if he followed. He did of course. He needed someone to talk to, and this strange fierce girl was better than no one.

He had had a book from Gran for his last birthday on how to paint portraits and he studied her face as she marched along the beach. Deep forehead, orangey eyebrows, eyes of a startling bottle-glass lightness, set rather close together, nose longish and bony, like the chin. It would be an interesting face to try and draw, he thought, with all those angles.

'D'you like living here?' he asked, to break the silence.

'Mmn. I like having the sea right outside the door. It changes every day. I'll be glad when my Dad gets back from Saudi though.'

'He been gone long?'

'Three months. He's an engineer. He had to go away to work when he got made redundant last year. We need the money. There's a lot of us to feed.' She grinned suddenly, showing slightly crooked teeth. 'Even vegetarians cost a lot to feed.'

'Are you *all* vegetarian?'

She nodded. 'All of us. Ma and Pa, sister Liza and my three brothers.'

Terry was impressed. He'd thought about it himself last year, hating the idea of animals being killed for food, but his mother had called it a 'modern fad' and in the end it hadn't seemed worth all the trouble it would cause.

'We drink milk though, and eat cheese and that.

Some vegetarians don't touch anything like that. They're called vegans.'

'Are they? That sounds like people from another planet.' She seemed to know a lot about everything he thought, or at least she sounded as if she did.

They reached the end of the pebble beach and the rocky headland towered above them. The beach was deserted except for a lone man and a dog. It was less popular than the sandy beaches further along the coast. Fiona remained silent and Terry kicked pebbles and thought about the conversation at breakfast that morning. His mother and father had been discussing Fiona's family. It was a popular talking point in a quiet seaside town where nothing much ever happened.

'The father's abroad apparently and now the mother has cleared off to Brownlea with those peace women,' his mother had said, pouring out coffee. 'Seems that the one with the bobbed auburn hair looks after them all, so the milkman said.'

His father held out his cup. 'How many of them are there?'

'Younger boys of seventeen, twins, and of course the girl of about thirteen in Terry's class *and* a boy in primary school. It seems downright irresponsible leaving a family that size to muddle along on their own.'

Terry, looking at the neatly set table with its clean cloth and gleaming china, had suddenly felt irritable. 'She's awfully good at Maths,' he said.

'Who is?' his mother asked, startled.

'The one in my class, Fiona.'

His father said, 'Yes, I played golf with your Maths teacher John Simms last week. He said she was gifted, already well ahead of her year. They haven't had a

11

chance to assess her properly yet, but she's definitely exceptional.'

'That's surprising,' his wife said.

'I don't see why she shouldn't be good at Maths just because her mother doesn't want to be blown up,' Terry said crossly, and ignoring his parents' exchanged glances, left the table without finishing his toast.

Outside, the first day of the summer holidays had begun, grey and draggy. He felt miserable. No good taking it out on his mother because he was upset over Zebedee. And Gran. He closed his mind over the thoughts. He didn't want to think too much about Gran.

The fate of the little donkey weighed heavily on him. Zebedee had lived in the field behind his house ever since he could remember, and he couldn't imagine life without the stumpy grey creature trotting to meet him for a carrot every morning. In his bedroom Terry had a pile of pencil and oil-crayoned sketches that he had drawn of Zebedee over the years. He stopped by the gate and whistled, pulling a carrot out of his pocket. The donkey came shambling across the rough grass. For years it had just been a two-acre paddock. Now, overnight, it had become a 'Desirable Building Plot' worth thousands of pounds, so his dad said.

Zebedee rested a heavy head on his shoulder and waited patiently for a titbit. Terry laid a hand along the bumpy spine, tracing the darker line of the cross marked there, feeling the bone, hard beneath the fur. He searched for signs of age and found them in the scraggy neck and the deep hollows over the mild eyes. Funny, he hadn't really noticed them until today. He had given the donkey a last pat and then wandered towards the beach. What else could he try? The RSPCA man had been kind, but not much help.

'He's an old donkey, lad. It's best for him to have a quick end.'

The people at the Riding School were sympathetic but matter-of-fact. 'It costs twenty pounds a week for stable livery, even if we had room, which we haven't.'

No one wanted to know about an elderly donkey. He'd looked round carefully and then kicked the Estate Agent's board hard. It stated in bright red letters:

SALE OF LAND BY AUCTION
2.2 ACRES.
AUGUST 7TH AT 'ROYAL OAK'
OUTLINE PLANNING FOR SIX HOUSES
APPLY REDRUP & JOHNSON

Now, standing looking at the sea with Fiona, he felt comforted by the fact that he wasn't, after all, the only one who cared. She broke the long silence.

'What else have you tried?'

Terry told her about the RSPCA man, the Riding School and the farmers who didn't want to know. The waves shuffled the khaki seaweed about and then receded, leaving patterns in the shingle.

Fiona lifted her head like a golden retriever pointing. 'The Island!' she yelled, flinging a long arm out towards the green outline, two hundred metres off-shore.

'What about it?'

'Ferryman's Island. Soon it'll be the Spring tides, some of the lowest in the year. Josh and Larry told me all about it. The causeway will be completely uncovered for a few tides. I read about it in the

13

paper as well. We'll check the times and take him across at night. Then, by the time anyone notices, the tides will have changed and he'll be safe. They won't be able to get him back!'

'Don't be daft,' Terry said. 'You can't hide a donkey. He'd never make it, he'd fall over. It's all covered in seaweed. And even if he did, someone would see him. Anyway, it'd be stealing.'

'And killing him would be murder. Which d'you think is worse?'

Terry was beginning to wish he hadn't told her. She was awfully bossy. He hurried along behind her as she loped back towards the cottage at the far end of the beach, thinking about the causeway deep beneath those threatening waves.

'Where are we going?' he asked.

'We've got to make plans. There's lots of things we need to find out. Times and the levels of the tides, the phase of the moon. All the kind of stuff my brothers are working on luckily. And we'll have to go out to the island ourselves first . . . .'

'Now wait a minute!' Things were getting out of hand.

'. . . then there's torches and things.' She was walking so fast, he almost had to run to keep up with her and his glasses were getting steamed up, blurring his vision.

'It just isn't possible,' Terry said, taking his glasses off and wiping them clear with the end of his tee-shirt.

She stopped walking suddenly and turned on him. 'How d'you know? You're just being defeatist without even thinking about it. It's going to happen! You and me are going to *make* it happen!'

Without waiting for him to answer, she hopped over

14

the low broken sea-wall and made for the cottage.
'Come on!'

Terry stared after her and then turned and looked
at the island, clear-cut beneath a brooding rain-filled
sky. He could picture Zebedee grazing on the close-
cropped turf quite clearly.

What he couldn't picture was getting him there.
Leading him across the squelching layers of weed,
around water-filled pools and sharp-edged rock, the
sea moving and threatening just a few metres away.

He turned to the open door of the cottage. He
would have to tell her, before this went any further,
that he was absolutely *terrified* of water.

You Can Hide a Donkey

The cottage was shabby with flaking whitewashed walls and deep windowsills. The open door was split in two like a stable. Outside was a small dinghy upturned on the grass. He read the name *Spinthrift* painted on the stern. On a patch of wasteland outside the gate a minibus was parked, its rusty metal disguised by bright blue paint decorated in huge white and yellow buttercups and daisies. He was attracted by the bold shapes and colours and stood studying them. Fiona came back out of the cottage.

'Come on Terry, we've got things to do.'

'Who painted that?'

'My younger brother Rufus. He's into colour. You'll like him. You're good at art, aren't you?'

He was surprised she'd noticed. He never got very good marks in class. Mr Carey, the Art teacher, didn't approve of his methods. Come to that Terry didn't approve of Mr Carey, but wasn't in a position to argue with him. Next year, when he moved into the third form, with a bit of luck, he'd change Art teachers.

'It's one of my two good subjects — that and English.'

'I've only got one — Maths.' She went back inside and he followed her. The door led straight into a large kitchen-*cum*-living room, which seemed to be filled with people and noise.

Fiona said loudly, 'This is Terry. We're making plans to save a donkey from being killed.'

A big girl with a cap of gleaming auburn hair stopped typing long enough to smile and say, 'Hi, Terry.'

Two lanky boys with very curly ginger hair looked up from a chart they had spread on their knees on a massive settee. They were arguing, but broke off to say, 'Hi' and 'Lo there' before carrying on loudly with their dispute.

A smaller boy on his knees beside a tin bath in the corner of the room looked up and smiled without saying anything. He was washing something coloured a vivid blue. That must be Rufus, Terry thought.

No-one said anything about the donkey. Terry, trying to imagine his mother's reaction if he just walked in and announced the same thing, grinned inwardly. He moved closer to see what Rufus was doing. The boy held out a deep blue bottle, still dripping from the bath. 'Poison,' he said.

'Eh?' Terry took the wet bottle cautiously. It was six-sided and had NOT TO BE TAKEN in raised capitals on one side, and deep ridges of raised glass on the others. 'It's a super colour.' The light revealed marks in the glass.

'Tears those are called,' Rufus said, pointing them out. 'Flaws in the glass.'

'Where did you get them all?' Terry looked at the rows of bright bottles lined up along the windowsills. Greens and browns and blues, with an occasional milky clear one.

Rufus had to raise his voice above the quarrelling twins.

'Different sites. I'm working in an orchard right next to a farmhouse at the moment. They're Victorian. Families used to dump their rubbish in odd corners — anywhere handy. I've got books about it if you'd like to see.'

One of the twins was saying something about salinity which Terry thought was something to do with salt. The other answered more quietly. 'You can't just ignore the dangers of water quality distribution and the chain effect.'

The big girl, Liza, just went on typing.

'Come on Terry, we've got work to do,' Fiona said impatiently. He would have liked to ask Rufus more, but he handed back the poison bottle.

'Thanks. I'd like to see the books.'

He followed Fiona into a tiny bedroom on the ground floor. It was bare and whitewashed and contained bunk beds and very little else. She gestured to him to sit down, and kneeling, rummaged in a cardboard box that she pulled from under the bottom bunk.

Through the open doorway he watched Rufus reach into his haversack for another bottle. Fiona followed his gaze. 'He's got loads of them,' she said. 'He's been collecting them for ages. He reads up about them to find out how they coloured the glass and things like that. It's the medicine ones he likes best.'

As she spoke she took a notebook and pen and sitting beside him on the bed, made out a list, printing untidily.

1 Distance from field to Island.
2 Dates and times of lowest tides.
3 Phase of moon on those nights.
4 Test donkey's walking speed.

Then she paused and chewed the end of her pen.

'We can check on the weather nearer the date. When did you say the sale was?'

'It says August the seventh on the board, but Zebedee could go before then.'

'Two weeks away. Is there anything else you can think of?'

'What about water? He drinks a lot. There's a big bathful in his field.'

'I never thought of that. How much d'you reckon he drinks a day?'

'About twenty litres at least — maybe more.'

'We'll have to ask Josh and Larry to help then. They could take water out in the *Spinthrift*. But we'll need some sort of tank by this afternoon, then if one of them will take us out we'll do a reccy later to make sure it's suitable and deliver it at the same time.'

Terry's stomach lurched. She was serious! This wasn't just some game to while away a flat day. Well, now was the time to tell her that no way was he going to cross that unfriendly stretch of grey water. He liked the sea well enough, but right there on the beach where he could keep an eye on it. He opened his mouth but Fiona jumped up and went into the living room before he could speak.

'Larry, Josh, can you help us? We need to get across to the Island to take a water tank over there. It's for this donkey we're saving from being slaughtered.'

Terry sat on the bed and waited for the twins to pour scorn on the idea. He didn't know much about families, being an only child himself, but he knew enough to feel confident that between them, Fiona's big sister and twin brothers, they would put an end to this mad scheme.

'I don't see why not. I've got to go out this afternoon in the boat while Larry goes to the library.'

Terry frowned and stood up. What kind of family was this?

Back in the living room he looked hopefully towards the wooden kitchen table where Liza was still typing. Surely *she* would say something? She was the oldest and supposed to be in charge of them. But all she said, without looking up, was, 'Make sure you all wear life-jackets.'

Life-jackets! It would take more than a life-jacket to make him feel safe. He was the only boy in his class who hadn't managed more than three strokes in the school swimming lessons.

Rufus, lining up more bottles on the deeply recessed windowsill where they caught and reflected the light, said to Terry, 'You can come with me and see where I dig them up one day if you like.'

'Thanks, I would.'

Fiona, who was perched on the arm of the settee looking at the chart the twins were studying, stood up, stretched and said, 'Come on Terry, it's time I met the condemned prisoner.'

Terry looked at the chart upside-down. It was a map of a coastline with lots of wavy lines showing currents and shaded areas that seemed to be water depths.

They went outside. 'You ought to feel honoured, Rufus would rather be on his own digging usually.' She gave him a fig that she had fished out of her pocket.

'I do.' He wasn't joking. He didn't often get invited places by other boys — even younger ones. He'd have

20

liked to admit that he'd far rather go and inspect the bottle-site than get involved any further with Fiona and her mad ideas, but he didn't have the courage. They walked in silence towards the donkey's field.

'You are free this afternoon?' Fiona asked, nibbling her fig with rabbity teeth.

'Er, yes,' he said reluctantly. 'My mother is going to visit my Gran in hospital. She's very ill.' He could have said he was going with her, only it wouldn't be true. It would have got him out of trouble nicely but he didn't like to use Gran's illness for that.

He felt the familiar misery return, thinking about his cheery little Gran all tidy in a white hospital bed. He didn't feel he had enough relatives to be able to spare any. He thought of all Fiona's brothers and sisters and sighed. It wasn't much fun being an only child.

'How old is she, your Gran?' Fiona asked.

'Eighty-eight.'

'Is she dying?'

He stopped chewing *and* walking, shocked by her question. His mother and father never used that word. Even when Grandpa had died they said, 'Passed On' or 'Gone To His Rest' — things like that.

'I suppose she might be,' he said slowly.

'Hadn't you ought to be going with your ma then?'

'She said she'd rather I didn't. She says she wants me to remember my Gran as she was.'

'How can you remember her as she was when she still is?'

Terry didn't answer. Really, she was a very odd girl.

'This is Zeb's field,' he said. Zebedee ambled across and stood regarding them over the gate, one ear

21

drooping and a faint gleam of hope in his eye at the thought of more carrots. 'I live in that house over there.'

'Mmn. Nice. Big, isn't it, for three of you?'

'It didn't seem big when Gran was home.'

'Hello Zebedee.' Fiona rested her hand on the scrappy mane. 'Have a fig.' The donkey curled back his rubbery top lip and picked the fig neatly off her outstretched hand. Terry laughed at the surprised expression on his face as he chewed.

'I've never met a fig-eating donkey before,' Fiona laughed, scratching his muzzle.

The sun shone fitfully through straggly clouds. She looked around at the ground which was rough and littered with stones, weeds, and coarse clumps of couch grass and ragwort.

'It's awfully bare here, he'll be much better off on the Island. I bet there's far more grass.'

Terry's stomach churned again. Now. Say it now. This was the moment to back out once and for all, but no words would form.

'Well, I'm off to beg, borrow or steal a water tank, see you later!' She gave the donkey a final pat and set off down the road with her loping stride and her dated ragged jeans flapping in the wind.

Terry took off his glasses and polished them. By the time he put them back on she was a tiny figure in the distance. He just wouldn't turn up. Would she come looking for him? Why had he pointed out his house?

He slid over the gate and wrapped his arms around Zebedee's neck. In spite of himself a bubble of excitement rose inside him. 'How d'you fancy a summer holiday old feller?' I reckon we might just pull it off, he thought. With Fiona.

Ferryman's Island

Terry clutched the smooth wooden sides of the dinghy. The water seemed to be knocking on the bottom of the boat trying to get in. He couldn't pull his mind away from the thought of all that cold grey depth below him.

He had arrived at the cottage after lunch determined to explain. It wasn't that he didn't *want* to help, he would say, or that it wasn't a good idea. It was just that, for *him,* it wasn't on. Water just wasn't his element. After all it was quite reasonable. Some people didn't like heights, or confined places. With him it was water.

Only, when he'd arrived, she was sitting on an upturned galvanised tank looking out to sea, looking smug.

'Where'd you get it?' he'd asked admiringly and she'd given him her crooked grin.

'Right behind the cottage catching rain-water off the roof. I've cleaned it out — it took ages getting all the green stuff off.'

'But won't your Dad mind, or your Mother?'

'Not when I tell them what it's for, anyway they're not here, are they? And it's not raining at the moment. We'll get hold of a barrel or something by the time they get back.'

Then Josh had come out and thrown him a shabby

old life-jacket that didn't look as if it'd support a Jack Russell let alone him, and somehow he'd found himself climbing stiffly into the boat.

Neither Fiona nor Josh seemed to notice how scared he was. Fiona sat in the bows, the tank jammed against her legs, staring ahead at the Island, the keen wind tangling her long hair.

Josh rowed with steady, cutting strokes, sending the *Spinthrift* skimming through the choppy waves, his thin muscled arms bare.

'We have got an outboard,' he was saying, 'but Larry says this is a good way to stay fit so we keep it for emergencies.'

Terry flinched at the word. He was afraid to speak in case his voice gave away how terrified he was.

'Nearly there.' Josh turned the bow of the boat at a different angle. 'I can use the tide now.'

'Larry and Josh know all about tides.' Fiona glanced over her shoulder pushing the red strands out of her eyes. 'That's what they're working on — tides and electricity.'

'Clean power,' Josh said. 'Down with filthy nuclear waste. If only governments spent a bit more time and money encouraging firms to *save* electricity, we wouldn't need to produce more and more all the time.'

'Lay off, Terry doesn't want to listen to all that stuff. He's only interested in drawing animals and birds, aren't you Ter?'

'The only trouble is, if they *do* build a barrage across the mouth of the river there won't be any birds for him to draw. Not the waders anyway. The mud at the mouth of the river is their feeding ground.' Josh sighed.

'Larry says, better a few hungry birds than nuclear

waste being dumped into the sea or into third world countries,' Fiona said.

At that particular moment, Terry, struggling not to be sick over the side, couldn't have cared less who dumped what where, or if he ever drew another bird in his life. He could feel himself turning green, sweating in spite of the cold wind. Imagine the humiliation of actually throwing up in front of Fiona!

The longing to feel firm ground beneath his feet made him dumb with misery. Why, oh why, hadn't he had the guts to *tell* them he was terrified of water?

After what seemed a lifetime, the boat scraped onto the tiny shingle beach on the leeward side of the Island. Fiona jumped out into the shallow water and grabbing the rope held the boat steady. Then Terry clambered awkwardly after her, his trainers soaked as he splashed thankfully ashore.

'You ought to have left your shoes behind like me,' she puffed, as she helped Josh to pull the boat up the shallow incline. But Terry was too relieved to be ashore to care about wet shoes.

The brother and sister worked like a team, obviously well used to boats. Josh wasn't a bit like Terry had imagined an older brother would be with a younger sister. He didn't say things like, 'I hope you kids know what you're doing!' or 'Mad idea, better forget it.' Instead he lifted the heavy tank out of the boat and set it down on the rocky shore. 'Well, where d'you want it?'

'We're not sure yet. Terry and I want to look around. How long have we got Josh?'

''Bout half an hour. You shouldn't need that long, it's not a very big Island.' He settled himself on the ground, leaning against a smooth rock, and taking a flute-like instrument from the haversack he was carrying, unwrapped it and began to play.

As Terry and Fiona walked up the shingle onto the larger rocks, the haunting notes floated after them, mingling with the wind, so that Terry couldn't tell where the tune ended and the wind began.

'Is that a flute he's playing?' he asked.

'Yes. It's a new one. He sold just about everything he owned to buy it.'

'Can Larry play as well?'

'No. Josh composes as well as playing. He reckons Music and Maths are the same thing to him. Larry can't understand it. That's one reason they're always arguing I think.'

'Are they very expensive then?'

'Depends. You can get cheap ones but that's a Rudall Carte.'

'A what?'

'That's the make of it. I don't know anything about them except that they're made of some special wood called cocus and some bits have to be made of silver to stop them from cracking.'

'Silver! No wonder they're expensive.'

'I expect it's the workmanship as well.'

They reached the grass and paused. Fiona wriggled her long toes in the green softness of the turf while Terry pulled off his wet trainers.

'Plenty for him to eat anyway,' Fiona said, bringing him back to reality. They walked on until they reached the highest point where they stood and looked around them.

The Island was wedge-shaped, about four hundred metres long and mostly grass covered. It rose gently at the southern end and shelved down to the sea where the grass changed to rocky pools and then shingle.

'I suppose you've been here lots of times?' Fiona asked.

'Well, actually . . .' Terry took off his glasses and polished them vigorously '. . . no.'

She didn't take him up on it. 'I've been here with Josh and Larry a few times but I've never looked at it with donkey eyes before.'

'Eh?'

'You know. As if *I* was a donkey myself. Now what would I need? Shelter, water, food. No dangerous cliffs. No point in saving him from the knacker's just for him to fall over and break a leg, is there?'

'There aren't any real cliffs here. It's a very gentle sort of Island.' Terry looked around consideringly.

'Still, he has been used to one flat field for most of his life and there *are* risks here. The thing is, ought we to take risks for him?'

'He's quite sure-footed. I mean, donkeys are, aren't they? And what else can we do? They may come for him any day now. P'raps they won't want him in the field when people are looking round it.'

'I suppose we could go and ask this Mr Fells to give us a bit of time to find somewhere else,' she said.

'I don't know exactly where he lives, anyway he might say no.' Perversely, the less keen Fiona seemed to be, the more he put his own fears to one side. 'You're not chickening out, are you?'

Fiona gave him her straight look. ''Course not dopey. I'm just thinking of all the angles, like where he can live after. You tried those Homes For Aged Horses places?'

'Not yet. They were my next try.'

'Well, he can't stay here all winter, there's not enough shelter and no-one to provide water because the twins will be at Cambridge. We'll have to get somewhere lined up ready if we do pull it off. We're not just here to enjoy ourselves,' she added severely.

Terry thought that if she knew how he felt about going back in that damn boat, she'd realise that enjoying himself didn't come into it! But he said nothing.

'Come on, we'd better get back to Josh.'

As they made their way back, avoiding thistles and sea-holly with their bare feet, he asked, 'Did you find out the dates of the next lowest tides?'

'July 26th or 27th will do. We could do it either of those nights. Can you get out about midnight?'

'I expect so.' Terry hadn't had time to consider details. He'd been too busy surviving the journey. Now he was back on firm ground, the urgency of getting Zeb away from a field that had become a death-cell really hit him.

'We'll put the tank over here by this old stone hut, shall we? There's some shelter in that corner where the walls are still standing. I expect it was from when they farmed here. They used to keep sheep and bring them over to the mainland to market in open boats,' Fiona said.

The notes of the flute rose and fell like some sea creature, lonely and sad. Then the tune speeded up, each note separate and clear, the same phrase repeated, over and over again. They stopped to listen, caught up in the haunting quality of the music. Then Josh came walking towards them.

'Well, made up your minds? D'you want this tank put somewhere or not?'

'Yes please. Over by that bit of wall.' They helped to carry it, stumbling over the rocks, and when it was in position returned to the boat. Josh pushed *Spinthrift* into the deeper water. Terry climbed

28

aboard, struggling to look unconcerned, and settled himself stiffly, heart hammering, fists clenched.

'How long are you planning to leave him there?' Josh asked.

'Can't be later than September and the last low tides.' Fiona settled herself comfortably in the bows again.

The trip back seemed mercifully shorter to Terry, with a cross-current pushing them along. He admired the ease with which Josh handled the craft. It couldn't have been light with the three of them in it. When they beached he nearly fell out in his anxiety to be on dry land again. He helped Josh to pull the boat well clear of the water and then stood watching him fixing the anchor ropes. Fiona walked up the beach towards the cottage.

'You don't like the water, do you?' Josh asked conversationally.

'I . . . how did . . .?'

'Feel the same way about caving. Fellow I know took me pot-holing once. Reduced me to a mass of pulp.' He grinned at Terry then slung a friendly arm around his shoulders. 'We're all scared of something, but not everyone's got the bottle to go ahead and do it anyway. You'll do.'

Terry stood for a moment looking after him, feeling about six feet tall. Then he followed them both up the beach, grinning. 'You'll do.' He liked that.

The Plan

During the next few days Terry and Fiona spent a lot of time in Zebedee's field. Every morning Terry dashed to the window and sighed with relief when he saw him still there, head down, grazing in the early morning light. He didn't really think that Mr Fells would spirit him away in the middle of the night, but somehow he only felt safe when he had the donkey in sight.

His mother, still involved with daily visits to the hospital, was unusually good about him going off every day, glad that he had found a companion, even though he suspected she didn't really approve of his choice. He still hadn't brought Fiona home, knowing that his mother would ask her embarrassing questions.

'I hope you aren't too disappointed about us having to cancel our holiday this year,' she said one morning. They went to a farm guest-house every summer in Dorset where his mother lazed about chatting to other guests, his father played golf, and Terry set off every morning with his sketching pad to draw the farm animals and wildlife. She would be surprised, he thought, if she knew how relieved he was about the cancelled holiday. 'When Gran is, er, better or whatever, we might fit in a week somewhere,' she said, coming as near as she ever had to admitting that Gran might die.

'When can I come with you to see her?'

'Well, dear, she's not . . . she's very weak, she's . . . I'll have to speak to Sister.'

Terry left it there. He wanted to tell Gran about Zebedee. Gran loved all creatures and they loved her. She had a robin so tame that it fed from her bedroom windowsill while she sat nearby. He could imagine her approving 'The Plan', chuckling over it and keeping it secret. 'My merry little Gran' was how Terry always thought of her, the old-fashioned Christmassy word fitting her perfectly. Most people's grans were either old and grumpy or too young and smart. He thought his Gran was just right. Short, dumpy and muddly. Her room had been the only one in the house filled with things that were just 'things'. Shells and fossil rocks, pieces of sparkling quartz and perfect bird feathers. He could hardly bear to go in there now that his mother had tidied everything away. At first, when his Gran had gone into hospital, he used to creep into the dead room to put crumbs out for the birds, but even so the birds had stopped coming now she was gone.

Gran would like Fiona. He could imagine the two of them together and Gran's bright eyes peering at Fiona's face and her sharp satisfied nod as she said, 'Now there's a girl. She'll do!' Like Josh had said to him, 'You'll do.' He felt a bit better.

'You'd like my Gran,' he said to Fiona. They were sitting on the coarse grass in a corner of Zebedee's field, leaning their backs against his open-ended shed. Zebedee grazed nearby and Fiona had her notebook out as usual, checking over details of 'D For Donkey Day'.

'Yes, I expect I would.'

31

'She's not a bit like my mother. She likes everything, birds, animals, insects even.'

'Can she draw them like you?'

'No. My Grampa could though. I expect I got it from him. He was nice too, but quieter than my Gran. She's a real good laugh. Grampa died two years ago. That's when Gran came to live with us.'

'I'd like you to show me your drawings.'

'Yes, okay.' It mattered so much that she liked his drawings that he was scared to actually show them to her. He didn't know why, after all she couldn't draw herself, but it did. It was nice having her for a friend, but he didn't think his parents really approved even though they'd never met her.

'No boys from school you're friendly with?' his father had asked the evening before. Terry wondered sometimes if his father would have preferred a son who played football and been good at golf, but if so he never said. The only times that Terry had been forced to play football he usually broke his glasses. But if he left them off, he couldn't see the ball. The other boys weren't exactly scornful, just left him to himself. He sometimes felt he'd have been given a rough ride if old Careworn Carey had made a favourite of him.

'You seem to be spending an awful lot of time with that girl,' his mother had said. 'What's her family like?'

'Oh, all right.' No prizes for guessing she wouldn't go over the top about the state of the cottage, he thought. But he loved it! Sitting on the edge of that cluttered kitchen table watching Liza preparing amazing looking things out of fruit and vegetables. Being teased by Larry and Josh about being hung as horse thieves. Helping Rufus to clean the bottles and

32

jars he dug up, watching the tears and bubbles appear in the imperfect glass.

Yesterday they had experimented with a new method for getting stains off different bottles. First they cleaned the outsides in a bucket of sand then tackled the insides by shaking gravel inside or soaking them in a bath of soda or a weak acid solution. Terry was impressed that Rufus was allowed to use chemicals without much supervision, but watching his careful methodical movements, he couldn't see that it was any riskier than someone older.

Terry got more and more interested in how glass was coloured and one day he'd gone with Rufus to the bottle-site on a nearby farm. 'D'you have to get permission to dig?' he'd asked as they climbed the orchard wall.

'Yes, and I have to tidy up the site when I've finished, but Mr Yeates — that's the farmer — is ever so nice. He comes and talks to me sometimes and tells me all about his grandfather and how they used to farm here.'

The site was carefully marked into squares with string in the corner where two stone walls met. Rufus had cleared the weeds, nettles and elder, dug over half of the marked area, and replaced the earth. They had spent a pleasant morning digging and found one good, green ink and an old wine bottle before replacing the soil. Terry was keen to go again some time, but at the moment his main concern was Zebedee.

All Fiona's family knew about 'The Plan' and that it was getting nearer every day, but even Liza said, 'Don't tell me any details then I won't have to tell any lies if anyone asks me. Just don't do anything stupid or dangerous.'

33

Josh said, 'They're both pretty sensible Liz, don't worry.'

Terry could tell the difference between the twins quite easily now, mainly by the way they spoke and acted. Larry was like a suppressed spring, coiled for action all the time. Terry was a little bit scared of him. Josh was slower, more quietly spoken with endless patience if you asked him a question.

In the field the sun made a brief appearance, slanting dusty rays from Zebedee's rusty coat. 'I'll be glad when my Gran comes home,' Terry said suddenly, pulling at the spiky grass.

'Mmn, I bet. There.' She put her pen behind her ear and handed him the notebook. 'Read that. See if there's anything else you can think of.'

Terry read aloud, 'One, full moon tomorrow and the tide is right. Two, tank filled with water and holds over sixty litres. Three, good torches. Four, rope halter and supply of carrots — are you bringing the carrots or me?'

'You. Tomorrow we'll go over in the daylight to check on how slippery it is, then if we think it's safe enough we'll take him the following night. Agreed?'

He wondered what she would do if he said 'No'. He nodded.

'And Josh and Larry will definitely go on delivering water?'

'They said they will, but perhaps I ought to learn to use the outboard in case of an emergency. I'd rather not have to rely on them. I wonder if Josh would let me?'

'If Zeb does drink as much as eighteen litres a day and if it doesn't rain much, we'll have to make a delivery every three days.'

'It's lucky for us that they're working on this tide thing. It means they're out in the boat every day.'

'What *are* they doing?' Terry asked. 'Josh tried to explain but he lost me in no time.'

'I don't understand it properly either but it's all to do with anti-magnetic pull to control tides so that the tidal flow can be used for electricity. When I go to Cambridge University like the twins I expect I'll work on the same thing.'

'How d'you know you'll get into Cambridge? You might not be clever enough,' he said, stung by her assurance.

She looked surprised. 'Oh, but I will. I mean, it's what my kind of brain is for, isn't it? It's got nothing to do with being big-headed.'

Terry changed the subject. There was a lot about Fiona and her family he didn't understand. 'D'you reckon I ought to go and visit my Gran, even if my ma doesn't want me to?'

He got her straight look. 'I think you ought to go and see your Gran when *you* think so, not anyone else. Come on, let's give Zebedee a good grooming ready for his journey.'

Terry followed her slowly across the field. I'll go and see Gran after we've moved Zebedee to the Island, he promised himself. Then I'll tell her all about it. He wouldn't admit that he was afraid of the things he sensed his mother wasn't telling him.

They fetched brushes and a halter and worked on the donkey's summer coat while he stood, head drooping, enjoying the sensation of the scratching bristles.

'His ears look too big for his head, his head looks too big for his body, and his body looks too big for his feet,' Fiona said, laughing.

Terry rubbed the bony head affectionately. 'I wonder what I'd need to mix to get that exact shade of fawn?' he said, stroking the smooth mealy fur around his muzzle. 'I've started using oils but they're dead expensive.'

'Start selling your drawings and make some money that way.'

'How d'you know they're good enough?'

'I've seen your class drawings. They're good.'

'Mr Carey doesn't think so. Old Careworn we call him. He's a miserable git.'

'He's a prat.'

'He doesn't like my methods. When he stands behind my chair my fingers freeze up and I can't draw anything.'

'Never mind, you'll be shot of him next year.'

'You can't blame him I s'pose. He said if everyone used up paper like me, trying to get it right, he'd run out of funds first week of term.'

'*You* aren't everyone,' Fiona said simply. She slipped the halter off the donkey and straightened his ears for him. He drifted away, pulling disinterestedly on the rough grass.

'I sure hope he likes living on the Island,' Fiona said, with a confidence of success that Terry didn't share. What about all the things that could go wrong? What if Zeb disappeared before July 26th. Or Mr Fells found out . . . or his mother? Or . . . anything?

Trial Run

The next day the lowest point of the tide would be midday. Terry, asking his mother for a packed lunch, said, 'Egg or cheese please,' thinking that he could hardly offer to swop sandwiches with Fiona if she gave him corned beef.

He set off with the familiar butterflies in his stomach. They had worked out the time of the tides together and then had their calculations confirmed by Josh and the local paper, but he felt no confidence in the sea sticking to the rules. It was a wild animal to him, subject to nothing but its own whims.

'You done any sketching lately?' Fiona asked when he arrived at the cottage. She was pulling on her battered trainers.

'Not since we got started on "D for Donkey Day". I brought my pad today though. My ma's noticed and I don't want her getting any ideas.'

'Noticed what?' She was trying to poke the chewed end of the shoelace through a hole.

'Noticed I don't go out sketching. She asked me where I was off to today so I said, "drawing".' He didn't mind the idea of working when Fiona was around. He'd bet she wouldn't stand looking over his shoulder watching, like some people — even complete strangers — did sometimes.

'You must keep at it,' she said seriously. 'It's your

37

thing. You still haven't shown me any of your drawings. I like the ones you do in school even though none of them are finished.'

'There's never enough time in school, I hate working to bells. I'll show you my other ones soon.'

'Damn, another lace gone!' Fiona held up the two broken pieces of lace, scowling. 'After all the time it took threading the flamin' thing too.' She disappeared into her bedroom leaving Terry alone with Liza who was writing, her pad on a corner of the cluttered table.

'There.' She stuck her pen behind her ear and smiled at Terry. 'Finished. Another article about Amnesty for one of the glossies. I hope!'

'What's Amnesty?' Terry asked.

'It's a group of people trying to help others who are in prison, or being badly treated by governments or dictators, in different countries.'

Terry liked Liza. He liked her straight unfussy ways and the wide smile she gave him when he came in. She had brown eyes and her dark auburn hair was cut in a short, fringed page-boy bob. He'd have liked to have had a sister like Liza. He didn't even mind when she got mad, which she did when the cottage got too messy and she had to stop writing and tidy up. He liked being included in the mad bursts of activity as she chased them round making them all help. It made him feel one of the family.

'D'you always write about Amnesty?' he asked.

'Nope.' She massaged her neck and stretched. 'I write about all kinds of things. Battered wives, force-fed geese, factory farming and where have all the tadpoles gone? Why do we blind rabbits for silly women to lacquer their hair?' She laughed. 'I started young — younger than Fiona is now. My dad says I'm a bossy female who thinks she knows better than anyone else. A trying-to-do-gooder. Perhaps he's right.'

Terry, not quite sure what she was talking about, nevertheless felt flattered by the conversation. He always had the feeling when talking to Liza that, as far as she was concerned, there was no age gap, that he was just another person.

'D'you sell lots of your articles?'

She frowned. 'Not enough. One in ten — if I'm lucky, but it's a start. I should be in London really where it's all happening, not stuck down here without even a phone.'

Terry looked at her in surprise. To him Liza belonged here, like Fiona, loving it. Now he saw that she was restless, marking time, waiting . . .

'Perhaps when Mother . . . oh, here you are Fiona, I gather something is happening today, but you needn't tell me what. Just take care.'

Fiona had her hair caught back in a rubber band, and was wearing paint-stained jeans. Her shirt was torn and she had replaced the broken lace in her battered trainers with a piece of string.

'Don't let anyone from the authorities spot you,' Liza said with a grin. 'They'll take you in for care and attention the way you look.'

'Where we're going there ain't no authority but Time and Tide,' Fiona grinned back.

'Go on Terry. Time, Tide and Fiona wait for no man. Good luck!' And with that she pulled the cover off her typewriter and was lost to them.

They set off after checking the time on Fiona's watch. It was eleven thirty-two. She pulled the notebook out of her pocket and wrote it down. 'We'll time how long its takes and compare it with the journey back.'

It was exciting seeing the causeway appearing as the grey water receded. First the higher rocks in the middle and then a long sloping bit nearer the Island. Inching back, the tide exposed more and more seaweed-covered rock. They followed its progress. Clumps of bladder-wrack weed glistened greeny-black in the light. They trudged over its squeaking surface, watching out for holes or sudden drops that might snap a donkey's leg. The waves crept forward and retreated as if reluctant to give up any secrets.

'Magic isn't it?' Fiona hopped happily across a gully and then looked back to judge it for a donkey stride.

'What?'

'All that power. The moon pulling the water surface up into a bulge all over the world! Larry's really hung up on it. He's working on some way-out ideas. I'll be glad when I can catch up with them. Josh doesn't get much time to teach me now.'

Terry didn't answer. He kicked a loose rock and hurt his toe. He felt left out when Fiona talked in that way about her family. They were all too clever by half, he thought meanly. All this knowing where they were going and what they wanted to do. He couldn't even keep up with the other kids in his stream in Maths, let alone decide on a career!

'We should have worn wellies, my feet are soaking,' he said.

'Mmn, so are mine.' But she didn't seem to mind — probably wouldn't even have noticed if he hadn't said anything. They reached the sloping bit and were onto dry rock. They passed sea-lettuce and oar-weeds as they made their way onto higher ground.

Fiona looked at her watch. 'Twenty-five minutes, but waiting for the tide to drop slowed us down a bit. If we allowed an extra fifteen for Zebedee we'll have at least an hour in hand. Of course getting back without him will be quicker.'

'It'll be dark don't forget.'

'You're right. We'll allow an extra half hour. It'll still give us time to settle him and get back.'

They walked to the highest end of the Island. Bright grass rolled away from them and as the sun suddenly flooded the scene, drifts of sea-pinks, and yellow Tom Thumbs coloured the grass. Suddenly Fiona ran, with skinny arms and legs flying, she leapt down the slope and, flinging herself down onto the springy turf, rolled over and over until she reached the smooth grey rocks at the bottom.

Terry took out his sketch pad and drew rapidly, covering page after page, his mind's eye holding the images, then he walked down to where she lay gasping and spreadeagled in the sun.

'My word I needed that.'

Terry laughed. He had captured all that movement on paper. Usually he only liked drawing animals. He'd given up on portraits. He had to have movement or perhaps frozen movement. The curve of a slow-worm sunning itself on a rock. Cattle drifting slowly as they grazed. The terrier on the Dorset farm leaping for a stick. Muscles lying in wait for action. Limbs stretched and curved. Fiona had looked like a colt running, all legs, angles and light. He closed his pad, pleased with himself. Knowing the rough sketches were good.

'Time to eat our sarnies,' she said, sitting up and pulling hers out of her pocket, all battered and squashed.

Terry glanced at the sea. 'It's not likely to creep in early, is it?' he asked. He would have preferred to eat his lunch on the mainland, safe from that encroaching line of tide.

'Nups. It's not likely to wait for you but it won't cheat either. A strong wind off the sea will speed it up a bit, Larry says, and push it higher, but there's no wind today.'

They finished their food, threw scraps to surprised seagulls that wheeled and called overhead and then set off back along the grass until they reached the causeway. Small grey crabs scuttled away and the sun glinted on vari-coloured shells that covered the higher rocks on the shore. Periwinkles and deep blue mussels.

'You'd think there'd be other people out here, wouldn't you?' Terry said.

'Too busy shadow living.'

'How d'you mean?'

'It's what Rufus calls people who don't ever do anything but watch telly and go to bingo — things like that. Shadow-livers.'

'I quite like some of the stuff on telly,' Terry said defensively.

'Well, so do I — or I did when we could afford one. But you know what I mean, it's not just telly, it's sort of not really seeing or hearing anything.'

Terry wondered whether his own mum and dad would count as shadow-livers by Fiona's family. He didn't like the idea. His Dad worked hard making money for them all. Surely if he wanted to flop in front of the telly or knock golfballs into little holes it was up to him? It was odd, he thought, how Fiona and the rest of her family could be fun *and* irritating at the same time.

Fiona was lagging behind, poking about in pools. He wished she would hurry up. He didn't want to be seen hurrying but he longed to be safely back on the beach. He looked at the waves, lapping nearer and nearer, imagining them creeping up to his ankles, then his knees . . . he speeded his pace and then suddenly fell, hard onto the rocks. For a few moments he lay there stunned, his ankle twisted painfully and cold wet soaking through his anorak. It was like a nightmare re-run of what might happen when they were dragging a reluctant donkey along the path!

He got slowly to his feet, testing his ankle cautiously. It was all right, not broken — not even sprained. *This* time . . .

'Terry! Terry! Come and look at this.' She hadn't even noticed him fall! He got crossly to his feet and limped back to where Fiona was crouched over a pool. 'What is it?'

'Look at this fish. The size of it! It's got caught in the pool. Think how baffled it must be feeling, his whole big world suddenly shrunk down to a tiny prison. House arrest, and the poor thing doesn't know that in a few minutes the tide will be back and it will be free.'

A few minutes! Terry looked anxiously around. 'How long have we got?' He tried to sound casual, looking down at the frantically threshing fish.

'Plenty of time yet — we're all right.' But to his relief she stood up and followed him. Ten minutes later they were safely back on the beach, watching the waters merge over the rocky pathway.

'Goodbye little fish. Happy freedom,' Fiona said.

D for Donkey Day

D for Donkey Day. All the talk and planning hadn't prepared Terry for how scared he'd feel. It wasn't just the thought of the journey along the seaweed-covered causeway, leading a stumbling donkey. It wasn't even the panicky feeling of getting trapped halfway back with the tide flooding over them. He was scared of those things as well, of course, but it was the actual act of stealing that suddenly hit him.

Up until now Terry had only thought of themselves as rescuers. Now he started wondering what would happen afterwards. They were bound to be questioned when Zebedee was discovered missing, even if they weren't actually suspected. At least *he* was. He lived much too near the donkey's field not to be asked whether he'd seen or heard anything. And Mr Fells knew how fond he was of Zeb, because they'd often chatted when the donkey was being fed in the winter.

But, as he pulled his jeans on and crept downstairs with a thudding heart, he knew there was no backing out whatever happened. He strapped on his wrist watch. Twelve o'clock. It was easier than he thought it would be to get out of the house. His mother and father had gone to bed fairly early and everything was peaceful. He pulled his pillow sideways and rumpled the quilt so that if his mother did look in it would seem as if he was in bed. Then he let himself out of the back door, leaving it unlocked, and made his way to the shed where he had left a rope halter and a bag of carrots ready, earlier that day. He changed into wellingtons, leaving his slippers ready for when they were safely back — wishing it was all over and he was on his way back to bed. He pushed the carrots and torch into the pocket of his anorak and crept out of the gate and across the stony path to the field.

The moonlight cast silver-black shadows everywhere. He could not remember being out this late on his own before. A cat materialised suddenly, beside a tree, making him jump, and then disappeared just as quietly. He saw, outlined above the gatepost, the shape of Fiona's head, and sighed with relief.

'Everything all right?' she whispered.

'No problems.'

Zebedee, milky brown in the moonlight, stopped grazing and ambled across the field to see what was going on.

'Hi feller, coming walkies?' Fiona said, patting his neck. Terry slipped the halter over the donkey's head, poking the large ears through with difficulty. They dragged the gate open as quietly as they could.

'Shall we close it?' Terry whispered.

'We'd better, someone is bound to notice an open gate and come and check.' She dragged it shut and they moved off down the track, the donkey's hooves tip-tupping on the stones.

Everything was quiet. The moon was brilliant and there was very little cloud, and better still, as far as Terry was concerned, no wind.

'It's lucky everyone round here goes to bed early . . .' Fiona began and then halted suddenly in her tracks. Terry, leading Zebedee, stopped behind her and the donkey's head bumped her back. Loud across the still night air came the sound of voices.

'It's the house down the lane — the Owens. They must have had a party or something and people are leaving right now. Just our perishin' luck,' Terry said.

'Well, I hope the prats don't spend too long saying "Goodnight". We can't afford to waste any time.'

They stood motionless in the shadow of the hedge. If they were spotted they would be asked some very awkward questions! The Owens knew Terry and no way would they swallow any story about why they were out at midnight with Zebedee. After what seemed an age of shouts and laughter, Fiona said, 'Come on, we daren't wait any longer. They're never going home by the sound of it.'

'But we'd have to go right past their house. Unless . . .'

'Unless what?'

'There *is* a way round the back, over the fields, down the cliff track and then across the dunes — but it'll take longer.'

'It'll be less risky than being seen — come on!'

They turned, skirted the hedge until Terry found the gap he was looking for. He handed the halter to Fiona and forced his way through, holding back the biggest branches. Fiona and the obedient donkey followed.

They were in a wooded copse, the path overgrown with brambles, the light of the moon obscured by thickly leafed branches. Terry switched on his torch and shone it around.

'Keep it low,' Fiona warned. 'We don't want any tiddly party-people nosing about.'

Terry aimed the beam at the ground. 'There used

to be a better path than this. It's all overgrown now.'

'Lead on then.' It was hard work forcing a way through the undergrowth. Spiteful brambles pierced Terry's jeans and he felt blood trickling, warm down his leg. Once, a branch whipped across his face and they spent the next few minutes frantically searching for his glasses, terrified that Zebedee might plant a careless hoof on them. When Fiona did find them, unbroken, Terry put them on with a sigh of relief. 'Darn things — I'm as blind as a bat without them.'

'Just don't lose them on the way there. Coming back I can always put the halter on you and lead you,' she giggled. At last they emerged on the other side of the wood and out into brilliant moonlight. It lit a path across the calm sea. 'There you are Zebedee, pathway to the promised land,' Fiona said, giving him a hug.

Terry looked at the deceptive sea and thought how deep and cold it really was. He read the time using his torch. 'Half past twelve already!'

'We'd better get cracking, but we've still got plenty of time.' Fiona was unconcerned.

They followed the track downhill keeping to the grass wherever they could, then they were on the sand dunes where the going became slower. Finally they reached the beach and Zebedee crunched across the shingle, his head lifted and nostrils expanded as he smelt the sea air.

'He seems to like the smell of the sea. Perhaps he used to be a beach donkey once,' Terry said.

The causeway was completely clear of water. They had hoped to follow the tide out like the previous day to give themselves the maximum time, but the delay in the lane had cost them precious minutes.

With Fiona in front with the torch ready, and Terry

47

leading Zebedee, they started toward the Island. Zebedee placed a cautious hoof onto the causeway and stopped, turning his head to look at them enquiringly. 'Come on boy, it's quite safe,' Terry coaxed, half hoping he would refuse to move so that they could go back home.

'Give me a carrot,' Fiona said. Terry handed her a couple from his pocket. Zeb lowered his head and snorted at the seaweed. Fiona held the carrot an enticing three inches from his nose. He crunched the first one and then decided the second one was good enough to move for. He walked carefully onto the wet squelching surface, moving with increasing confidence as he went.

Fiona went on ahead with the torch, checking for sudden drops or holes. On either side the sea lapped and sucked, seeking hidden places, talking to itself. Zebedee stepped out boldly, looking about in surprise at this new environment.

'He likes it! This is fun,' she said, 'I love being out at night, don't you? Better take him left a bit here, there's a hole.' Terry didn't answer. *He* wasn't enjoying himself. He kept his eyes down, his imperfect vision battling with the distorting moonlight and the sea an enemy, only feet away from him. His insides were shaking, he longed to turn and run back to the safety of the beach.

They were about halfway across when Zebedee stopped. For no apparent reason he froze in his tracks and stood staring intently ahead, as unmoving as if he had been carved from stone.

'What's up?' Fiona called back from where she was checking a loose rock.

'Come on boy,' Terry urged, tugging at the rope. But the donkey stood rooted as firmly as if he had

48

grown from the ground. 'He just won't move,' he yelled to Fiona, trying to keep panic out of his voice. She came back, hopping confidently over the rocks to join him.

'Give him a carrot.' She pulled one from his pocket and Zebedee ate it eagerly, then she held another one inches from his nose, just out of reach. He stretched his neck and curled back his top lip but still didn't move.

'What shall we do?' Terry looked at the dark, threatening, moving line of sea.

'I could get behind and push,' Fiona said, not very hopefully. Of course it did no good. Terry pulled and she pushed and Zebedee fixed his hooves even more firmly into the wet seaweedy rocks.

Fiona stopped pushing. 'This is hopeless. The best thing we can do is to leave him.'

'Leave him!' It was the very last thing Terry thought she would suggest. He was terrified at their lack of progress but it hadn't occurred to him to abandon the donkey.

'Well there's no chance we can shift him by force, and time's running out. If we walk on towards the Island he may feel lonely and follow.'

'But what if he turns for home?'

'In that case we can chase after him. Anything's better than just standing here till we all have to swim for it.'

They set off, leaving the donkey standing looking after them, halter rope dangling. After they'd gone about fifty metres, Terry looked back. Zebedee, palely luminous in the cold moonlight, stood like a ghost. 'It's not working,' he said. 'What'll we do now?' Why had he even listened to this crazy girl?

Suddenly Zebedee threw up his head and gave a

raucous bray. It was the most shocking noise Terry had ever heard. It resounded around the quiet bay and erupted into the night. They clutched each other in horror, then started back towards him as he came after them, skidding far too fast on the treacherous surface.

Fiona reached him first and grabbed a trailing rope. She steadied him to a more sensible pace and said to Terry, 'Keep going, it might not work next time.'

Terry was sweating with tension. It was the one thing he'd never thought of, Zebedee just stopping. They made the last stretch in record time and led him thankfully over drier rock and then shingle.

'Phew, I wonder what that was all about,' Fiona said, pulling Zeb to a halt and leaning against him with relief.

'But if he won't leave us, how are we going to get back without him following us?' Terry said.

'There seem to be a few things we didn't think of on our trial run,' she admitted cheerfully.

Return Trip

They reached the grassy slope, glad to be clear of the slippery seaweed and rocks. Zebedee broke into a trot when he felt the springy turf under his feet. They ran, one on either side of him.

'He likes it here,' Fiona said.

'I've never seen him looking so lively. Shall we turn him loose?'

'P'raps we'd better show him round a bit first, but we haven't got much time left. We've taken much longer getting here than we planned.' She looked at her watch. 'We ought to be starting back in five minutes.'

They led the donkey to the water tank and he immediately put his head in and drank deeply. 'Don't drink too fast, that's got to last you three days,' Fiona said. They led him about before slipping the halter off. Terry put the last of the carrots in a pile next to the tank to keep him occupied. With one last hug and pat from each of them they left. At the start of the causeway they looked back but he was still happily chomping his carrots.

Already the causeway looked narrower to Terry. He scrambled over the rocks, anxious to cover as much ground as possible. Fiona splashed carelessly through deep pools, even though she was still wearing her battered trainers. When they reached the highest rocks about halfway, they stopped to look back. Zebedee was standing on the highest point, outlined in the moonlight.

'Tide's coming in fast, look,' Fiona said. Behind them the track was already blotted out and the water was creeping after them. In front, the path dipped and the sea was swirling across, surrounding them, as if in a hurry to meet. They increased their speed, jumping recklessly from rock to rock. It had all taken a lot longer than they had bargained for, what with not being able to go the lane way and then Zebedee turning stubborn. Terry's eyes watered with the strain of watching the menacing line of water and the treacherous shapes and shadows of rocks beneath his feet.

'Can you swim?' Fiona asked suddenly.

'No.' It was a question he'd always hoped she would never ask. 'Can you?'

'Yes.'

Did she think they might have to, for crying out loud? At the thought he stumbled, missing his footing completely, and fell heavily on the hard rocks like a recurring nightmare. Fiona, who was ahead, came racing surefootedly back when she heard him cry out.

'Terry! Are you all right?' Slowly and painfully he got to his feet. His leg was bruised and stiff but worst of all he had lost his glasses again.

'My goggles.'

Fiona shone her torch. 'Here they are! One lens is broken though.'

He felt sick with fear. The world blurred and shimmered as if he was under water already. Fiona pushed the broken glasses into her pocket, then thrust the end of the halter into his hand. 'Here, hang onto this, and keep behind me. Just try to put your feet exactly where I put mine.'

He hardly noticed the pain of his injured leg as he stumbled blindly behind Fiona. Ahead of them the waters touched and met. Fiona splashed determinedly through shallow pools, her eyes fixed on the beach ahead. Once, Terry, clumsy in his waterlogged boots, stumbled and almost fell, pulling her down with him, but between them they managed to recover their balance and stagger on. The water was up to their ankles and getting deeper rapidly.

'Only a bit farther,' Fiona puffed.

'My boots are like lead. They're full of water, I'll have to take them off,' Terry groaned, feeling the tug of the strong current knocking him off balance, the level of water rising up his legs. It was his worst nightmare come true. Fiona helped him as he hopped, half blind, fighting panic as the dark waves swirled around them. The boot wouldn't come off! The weight of suction against their frantic tugging almost bowled them over. At last the first one came free, then the water deepened suddenly, almost reaching their calves. It made walking almost impossible. His one boot was like an anchor.

'Come on!' Fiona grabbed hold of him and together they floundered the last fifty metres pushing against the bullying weight of the water.

Then they were in shallower water and flinging themselves across the shingle. Gradually Terry's heart stopped racing. 'Thanks Fiona.'

She sat up. 'We did it!' Jumping to her feet she turned a cartwheel.

'No thanks to me,' he said gloomily.

'Oh, stop whingeing. He's on the Island safe and sound, isn't he? Thanks to *both* of us. Now all we need is a few days, and then they won't be able to get him off even if they find him!'

She was right, he thought. They'd done it! The enormity of it suddenly hit him. He peered into the darkness where the waters swirled and met and his heart failed him.

'What if he drowns? What if he tries to get back next tide?'

'Honestly Terry, don't be such a wimplet! Why on earth should he when he's got all that gorgeous grass?'

'Well, he might fall off the edge.'

'Of course he won't. He's an *animal* with a sense of survival. There aren't any steep cliffs anyway. Besides,' she added practically, 'don't forget he was due for the chop, and drowning is supposed to be quite a pleasant death — better than a ghastly slaughterhouse.' Terry thought of fighting for breath before those choking waters closed over his head, and said nothing. Personally he'd choose a bullet between the eyes any day of the week! 'Pity about your glasses though.'

'I've got a spare pair. My ma will be mad though.'

'Any other damage?'

'I dropped my one welly — and the torch. I don't remember when.'

'Still, we didn't drown. I was scared stiff, were you?'

'Were you?' Terry felt comforted. 'I thought if you could swim it'd be different.'

'I'm not all that good a swimmer and anyway with the sort of currents you get round an island I don't think it would make much difference if you could swim or not.' She sat on a rock and pulled off her trainers. 'Ugh, I might just as well walk barefoot as

54

wear these, they've had it.' She threw a wet trainer into the air and caught it. 'I'll chuck them away and try to find a good jumble sale or go to the Oxfam shop tomorrow.'

Terry could feel the pain in his leg now that the exhilaration of their escape was fading. He got up stiffly and they stood and took a last look at Ferryman's Island, darkly mysterious in the moonlight. 'Can you see him?' he asked Fiona, cursing his own blurred vision.

'Just. He's still standing on the highest point. I hope he doesn't make a habit of *that*, it makes him too easy to spot. I bet he loves it there after all those years in the same field.'

'I hope he won't be lonely. He loves people.'

'It's only for a few weeks and he's used to being on his own after all. Come on, you'd better get back home.'

They limped along the shingle to where the dunes merged with grass. Further inland bramble bushes bordered the path. Fiona threw her trainers into the middle of them.

'Good compost. You may as well chuck your welly in, one's no good to you and I'll try and find you a pair in the jumble. What size do you take?'

'Sixes. But my mother will notice the difference. She notices everything.'

'Easy. Tell her you mixed them up in the school cloakroom. Shall I walk home with you in case you can't see where you're going?'

'No, I'll be all right, honestly.' But he was glad when she insisted and they set off, barefooted, their wet jeans clinging to their legs.

'How long d'you reckon it'll be before Mr Fells notices he's gone?' Fiona asked.

'He comes up to check the water once a week. Now the field is for sale, though, there's been people looking round it. Perhaps the agent will notice he's gone.'

'Unless he thinks he's already had him destroyed.'

'We'll just have to wait and see.' Terry gave a huge yawn, feeling suddenly exhausted. 'I just hope we have a few days to get our act together before the tides change. Once the Island is cut off again there's not much he can do, is there?'

'I hope he doesn't bring the police into it,' Fiona said. 'Though I wouldn't see any point in getting the police to look for a donkey you're going to have killed anyway.'

'I think Mr Fells cares about Zeb really.'

'Funny way of showing it.'

They trudged on for a while in silence, each busy with their own thoughts, Terry's feet weaving and tripping, through a combination of tiredness and poor eyesight.

When they reached the gate to his garden he whispered, 'I feel rotten now, you having to walk back on your own.'

'Well we can't very well keep walking each other back and forward all night, can we?' Fiona giggled. 'Anyway, I'm used to being on my own at night. I like it. I often go for long walks by the sea. See you tomorrow fellow donkey rustler. We'll have to think of a way to celebrate.' And she was gone.

Terry let himself into the quiet house, locking the back door carefully. He stood in the dark kitchen listening for any sound, but all was silent. With relief he eased off his soaked jeans and jacket and pushed them into the laundry basket, hoping, without much optimism, that his mother wouldn't question how they got so wet. Then he crept upstairs and, too tired to bother about his filthy feet and stinging, bloodied legs, fell into bed and immediately into a deep sleep.

The Day After

Terry's mother called him half a dozen times before he woke the next morning. The last time she shook him awake. 'For goodness sake, Terry, what's the matter with you? I've had a phone-call from the hospital. Gran's taken a turn for the worse. I've got to go.'

He jerked awake, head swimming, his mind a confused jumble of the events of last night and the news about Gran.

'What? What's the time? Can I come with you?' He swung out of bed, forgetting he'd crawled into bed in his underpants.

'Terry! Just look at the state you're in! Ever since you met that girl . . .' His mother stood with hands on hips looking furious and upset at the same time. 'No you can't come. I might have taken you if you'd been up and washed, but I can't wait now. Clean yourself up and put some antiseptic ointment on those scratches. I'll phone from the hospital when I've got some news. I'll see you when I get back,' she added threateningly and left without giving him a chance to answer.

He sat, dazed, on the side of the bed. Gran. A turn for the worse. What did that mean? His mother should have waited . . . but did he really want to go? Zebedee. What if Mr Fells came today. Could he lie convincingly? He reached for his glasses then, remembering they were broken, groaned and put his head in his hands. His ma was *not* going to be delighted when she got back.

Stiffly, he went and ran his bath, sprinkling in a liberal dose of Dettol. It must be good for cuts, he thought. Looking at his stinging legs and arms as he lay in the welcome warmth of the water, he could see why his mother had been shocked. Red weals stood out vividly against his fair skin and trickles of dried blood smeared the scratches. Where he had fallen on the rocks, purple bruises were forming from ankle to knee. He hurt all over.

After his bath he put on some ointment and dressed in clean jeans and shirt. Then he ate some cereal and mooched about miserably wondering whether Zebedee was safe and what was happening at the hospital.

Hopefully, what Zeb *wasn't* doing was standing outlined against the skyline for everyone in the town to see if they took a walk. If only they could explain to him that he must keep to the seaward side of the Island. Keeping a low profile — literally — until the tides changed.

He wished he could let Fiona know about Gran, cursing, not for the first time, the fact that they weren't on the phone. He daren't leave the house in case his mother rang. He would have loved to tell Gran about their adventure. He'd never had anything half as exciting to tell her before. What if Gran . . .? He jumped as the doorbell rang. Heart thudding, thinking it must be Mr Fells, he opened the door cautiously and Fiona stood there grinning. 'Hi partner. I saw both your parents' cars were gone so I took a chance.'

'Come on in!' He was delighted to see her.

'Everything okay?'

'Yes. No. My Gran is worse. The hospital rang and my mother has gone to see her. I'm waiting for her to ring.'

'That's rough.' She followed him into the kitchen. 'What did they say?'

'She's taken a turn for the worse.' He repeated the meaningless phrase automatically. 'Any sign of Zeb?' His fears over Gran were stretching to surround everything. Nothing could go right now.

'I don't think it'll be very long before someone spots him. He's perched on the high end doing his "Lord of all I Survey" act. Daft animal.'

'My mother saw my cuts and bruises as well. I don't think you'd better be here when she gets back. She thinks I'm keeping bad company.'

'She could be right. Is she very mad?'

'Not half as mad as she'll be when she finds out about my goggles. She doesn't know about *them* yet — only my legs. These are my spares.'

'I didn't realise you could get spare legs as fast as that.'

'Spare glasses, dope. They've got different colour frames so she's bound to notice.'

'I'll look out for some wellies at the jumble sale if you like. I've got to go for some trainers. I've only got these flip-flops left to wear.'

He made them orange squash and opened a packet of biscuits.

'Here you are. Let's hope my mother phones before she comes home. She's been dying to meet you. She'll ask you all sorts of questions about your family, I'm warning you. That's why I've kept you out of the way.'

'While I *am* here how about showing me some of your drawings?'

'Yes, okay.' He climbed the stairs slowly, not just because his leg hurt. He only showed his special drawings to Gran as a rule. And Grampa before he died. But he wanted Fiona to see them, not only because he felt he owed her something for not leaving him last night, but because he needed her to like them. Silently he laid the folio on the kitchen table and spread the pictures out.

Most of them were of Zebedee in the field. Terry had captured the donkey with light sure strokes. Zeb lying down, struggling to get to his feet after resting. Zeb, sleepy eyed in hot sunshine. Rolling in mud. The drawings jumped off the page, each economical line showing not just any donkey but Zebedee as only Terry knew him.

'Terry, they're good!' Fiona sounded excited. 'I knew they would be. That's why I was longing to see them, but I didn't realise *how* good you were.'

He blushed, then relaxed. He had known in his bones that they were good, but he needed to have her confirm it. She leafed through the rest of the pictures in the folder. Holiday sketches from the holiday farm in Dorset. A lively Jack Russell jumping for a stick, the farm collie flattened to the ground, alert, waiting for a whistled command, a black kitten fighting a tangled ball of wool, showing not cute kittenish ways, but the hidden tiger lurking in every cat.

'They're better than good, Terry, it's what you must do.'

'How d'you mean?'

'It's like me and my Maths, its . . .' She broke off as the doorbell shattered the peace of the kitchen. They stared at each other, both thinking the same thought.

'It can't be!' Hastily, Terry gathered the scattered drawings and pushed them into the folder. Together they went to the front door.

Mr Fells stood on the doorstep, large and red and *very* cross.

'Terry. Is your mother in?'

'No. She's at the hospital visiting my Gran.'

'Well, it's you I want to see really. Can I come in?' Terry led the way silently into the sitting room desperately wondering what to say. Why hadn't he and Fiona been getting their story together instead of wasting time looking at his pictures? They all sat down.

'This is my friend Fiona, Mr Fells,' he said, just in case Fiona hadn't realised who the man was.

'Where is he, Terry?'

Terry didn't answer.

'Where's who Mr Fells? Fiona asked brightly. He ignored her and went on looking at Terry.

'Do you mean Zebedee? Has he escaped?' Terry asked in a squeaky voice.

'I do mean Zebedee and no, he hasn't escaped. Donkeys don't close gates after themselves and since he's been perfectly content in that field for fifteen years I can't see him breaking out in his old age, can you?'

Terry stayed silent.

'But the field is going to be sold, isn't it?' Fiona interrupted in the same bright silly voice. 'Perhaps the donkey senses it and feels unsettled. Animals are supposed to have a sixth sense for things like that, aren't they?'

Terry, guessing she was playing for time to give him a chance to think, racked his brains in vain for something to say.

Mr Fells looked straight at Fiona for the first time and she looked right back with her fierce green stare. 'Young lady, I strongly suspect that both you and Terry know a good deal more about this business than you are prepared to admit.' Now they both remained silent.

'In answer to your question,' Mr Fells went on, 'yes, I do think animals have a sixth sense, but so do I, and at the moment *my* sixth sense is telling me that no donkey opens and closes a gate and takes himself off because he's telepathic enough to know that his field is up for sale.'

'And that he's going to be shot,' Fiona said quietly.

Mr Fells' face went redder than ever and beneath the moustache his mouth tightened. He turned back to Terry. 'I'm not informing the police — yet. I'm giving you till tomorrow to put him back in the field. If he's not back by tomorrow morning I'll come and see your parents and see if they can get some sense out of you. And the only reason I'm giving you that long is because I know you will have taken good care of him.'

'But what if you're mistaken and somebody else has let him out or stolen him?' Fiona pointed out in her ordinary voice.

'I'll take a chance on that. I'll be along to see *your* parents as well,' he added grimly and went to the front door without another word. They followed. Fiona whispered, 'I hope he's prepared for a long journey if he wants to see my Dad!'

At the door Mr Fells, turning to deliver a final warning, startled Terry into dropping the folder that he was still clutching.

One of the pictures fluttered to the ground and landed at Mr Fells' feet. He picked it up and stared at it. It was Zebedee, browsing knee-high in buttercups and thistles. The man's expression softened. He looked from the drawing to where Terry stood miserably in the doorway.

'Look lad, I love the old fellow too. We've had him over fifteen years. He was a pet for all my kids, and, well, they're all grown-up now, and he's very old. People owe a duty to their animals. Just one quick minute and then he'll never suffer like some old animals do. Shipped abroad for slaughter — I've seen some of what goes on and I know. You'll understand better when you're older.'

'You mean people stop caring when they grow up and there's money involved,' Fiona flashed. 'How would *you* like to be shot when *you're* old — just because you *are* old?'

'Young lady, your heart is in the right place, but there are, in fact, many elderly people who would be glad of a chance of just that. Maybe one day I'll be one of them, maybe I won't, but yours is far from being a foolproof argument.'

He put the drawing into Terry's hand and left. Fiona shut the door. 'He's okay,' she said, to Terry's surprise.

'Sorry I wasn't more help.'

She grinned. 'I'm just more chopsy and better at telling lies than you. It's my bad upbringing.'

'Anyway, I still think Zeb would rather be lording it over his very own island than getting his brains blown out,' Terry said.

'He can't have discovered where Zebedee is, or he wouldn't be trying to get us to talk. That gives us a bit of time anyway.'

'I wonder how he found out so fast that the field was empty. The agent I expect.'

'I wonder if he will tell the police? I'd rather stay out of real trouble while my ma is at the Peace Camp. It makes it look bad for Liza otherwise.'

'I bet he comes to see *my* mother anyway and it won't take her long to work out that I scratched my legs and broke my glasses the same night that Zebedee disappeared.'

'I'd better go. There's a good jumble in town this afternoon. I hope the news about your Gran is good. Lie low, admit nothing and we'll just pray that Mr Fells doesn't find out where Zeb is for a few more days.'

After she had gone, Terry put his folder of drawings away, thinking about what Fiona had said about them. 'It's what you must do, like my Maths.' Of course he would go on drawing, it was his hobby. Or did she mean for a living? His dad was always on about him becoming a solicitor or an accountant. 'Good solid living, always plenty of work.' But Terry couldn't imagine working in an office all day. It would be like school again, and anyway, he wasn't brainy enough.

He collected a new sketching pad and pencils and went downstairs to wait for the phone to ring, worrying afresh about Gran. To pass the time he tried drawing from memory, Fiona and Zebedee walking across the causeway. His hand moved, fast and sure, and Fiona appeared, ragged jeans, slightly too short, showing her ankles. Then her hair, tangled, lifting in the slight breeze. Then Zebedee, tail and head high. He drew rapidly, his mind's invisible eye was like a computer, absorbing and storing details until he needed them. He frowned in concentration, polishing his glasses and rubbing his eyes when he failed to capture the exact thing he wanted from his pencil, a kind of wildness that came from the girl, the donkey, and the atmosphere of the night, in spite of the still, calm weather.

For over an hour he drew, ripping out pages in exasperation when he wasn't satisfied until the floor around his chair was littered with crumpled rejected scrap. He knew it was wasteful but it seemed to be the only way he could work. In every other way he was clumsy and slow. Only with a pencil in his hand he seemed to know how to move, where to aim. At times his brain couldn't keep up and in despair he wrecked what others seemed to think adequate. It was one of the reasons he fell out with old Careworn in school.

He was getting nearer to what he wanted when he heard the key turn in the lock. His stomach gave a great lurch of fear as he realised it must be his mother back from the hospital. He had forgotten all about Gran! No, not forgotten, covered the fear over. Slowly he closed his book and went to meet her.

'Terry?' She looked drawn and tired but when she saw his face she said quickly, 'It's all right, love. Gran had a slight stroke in the early hours but she's making progress.'

'I'll get you a cup of tea,' he said, afraid to ask what 'having a slight stroke' meant. His mother looked awful, but not angry any more.

He brought the tea and set it down carefully.

'Thank you love. Terry . . . you do realise that Gran might not get better, don't you?' He nodded. 'She's very old.'

Like Zebedee, he thought. 'I'd like to go and see her.'

'She can't talk to you, she might not even recognise you.'

'She's still my Gran. I think I ought to go.' Suddenly he was quite sure.

'Yes, all right. You can come with me tomorrow. You and she were so close, such good friends, I wanted you to remember her always like that. But perhaps you're right.'

She stood up, her old brisk self again. 'Now. What on earth is all this paper doing on the floor? And why are you wearing your spare glasses?'

Bad News

Next morning, his mother phoned the hospital and learned that Gran had had a good night. As soon as he decently could, Terry escaped to call for Fiona. He didn't want to be around if Mr Fells came early to check on the field, and then came round to see his mother. He didn't think she believed him altogether when he'd said his glasses had fallen off and he'd stood on them accidentally.

The field looked oddly bare when he passed it. He felt a flutter of nervous excitement at the enormity of last night's action. He had told his mother before he left that he would be back in time to visit Gran with her after lunch. He only hoped nothing would happen in the meantime to spoil the arrangement.

Fiona was sitting on the low windowsill outside the cottage fiddling with a pair of binoculars. 'How's your Gran?' she called.

'She's no worse. They said on the phone she had a comfortable night. I'm going with my mother to see her this afternoon. There was no sign of Mr Fells so I got away fast. Where is everyone?'

'Liza caught the early train to London. She's got an interview about a job on a magazine. The twins had a nasty row and Josh went along the beach with his flute and Larry rowed off into the sunset.'

Terry glanced at her curiously. 'Eh? Bit early for

a sunset, isn't it? Where's Ruf?' She seemed flat and distracted. He had expected to find her bouncing.

'Gone off with his spade. He hates quarrelling. I've been trying to spot Zebedee with these things. I bought them at the jumble sale yesterday for twenty pence.'

'Anything else wrong?' Terry asked.

She didn't answer, just handed him an apple and went on peering through the binoculars. After a bit she said, 'Here, you have a go. If Larry had been in a better mood I was going to ask him to take us out to check on Zebedee. I haven't spotted him yet, and I'd like to make sure he's safe after his first night.'

Thinking of Mr Fells and the temper he'd been in, Terry silently agreed with her. He peered through the lenses but could only see a blur so he handed them back. 'What were the twins quarrelling about?'

'Oh, the usual. Conservation and clean power. Josh on his usual — if a barrier *was* built, it would flood the feeding ground of some wading birds. Can't remember the name.'

'I know them. Spotted Redshanks. They've only just been recorded here.' He had tried to capture them on paper, but it was hard to get near enough. Pale, slender wading birds, with white rumps that showed as they sifted the estuary mud with their long thin beaks.

'Yes. Well, Larry says he realises you can't alter anything as big as a channel without affecting all kinds of things, sea-life and stuff, but you win some, you lose some. Josh doesn't see it like that.'

'They've been arguing about this for ages. What blew it up this early in the day?'

She had her head down, fiddling with the binoculars. 'It's not just that. The *real* argument was about the cable that came this morning.' She stared at the binocular lenses as if they held some secret they wouldn't reveal to her.

Terry waited for a bit and then prompted, 'Cable?'

'From Saudi. It came this morning after Liza had left for the train so Larry opened it. Dad's had an accident and he's in hospital with concussion. Not serious — they *said*. He was out at one of the sites and something fell. The thing is, Larry doesn't want Ma to know till after this demo thing.'

'Did your dad send the cable himself? He can't be all that bad if he did.'

'It was from his firm. Ma rings Saudi every fortnight 'cause we're not on the phone here, and Dad can't ring the Peace Camp of course. Larry says not to worry Ma till this big demo thing is over. She's one of the organisers. But Josh thinks she ought to know.'

'So what are you going to do?'

'Wait till tonight when Liza comes home and see what she thinks. She'll be back on the last train.'

'Haven't you got a phone number you can ring in Saudi so you can find out how your dad is now?'

'Liza's got the number in her book and she's taken it with her, so we can't do much yet.'

'Do *you* think your ma should know? And Rufus, what about him?'

'*I* think what Ma is doing is important and if Dad's not seriously hurt — well — it'd be a shame to upset her. *Rufus* just wants Ma to come home.'

Privately, Terry thought this was quite reasonable. After all, it must be bad enough having your dad gone for months on end without your mother disappearing to some camp where she couldn't even be contacted without a lot of fuss. But he didn't think it a very good idea to say so out loud.

'Was your mother mad about your glasses?' Fiona asked.

'Not too bad. She seemed too tired to care. She's forgotten about the scratches on my legs as well.' He was wondering, not for the first time, what *her* mother was like. He had a picture in his mind of long skirts, big wooden bangles on thick brown arms and lots of wild red hair. Would Fiona be able to go on doing what she liked when her mum came back, he wondered? Not washing all that often, moonlight walks and jumble sale clothes?

'I got you some wellies, not wonderful, but they're the right size. And these — look!' She poked her feet out for him to admire her black and yellow trainers. 'It was dead good, the jumble. Conservative Ladies. You ought to see the things they chuck out! Don't tell Liza where I got them though, she'll say I'm supporting an obscene cause or something.'

They wandered to the edge of the sea and stared out towards the Island but there was still no sign of the donkey. The sea was empty of any craft.

'What do I owe you for the boots?'

'Have them on me. I made two quid helping Rufus lug some bottles to that secondhand shop in town. You know the one, "Bits & Bobs". We got four quid for four of those old pop-alley bottles, the ones they used to put ginger beer in with glass marbles in the necks.'

'Codds — that's what they're called.' Terry felt a pang of 'not belonging', wishing Rufus had asked him to go. As if she guessed, Fiona said, 'He likes me going with him 'cause I'm better at bargaining than he is.' She swung the binoculars by their strap

71

as they walked along the tideline. 'I think these must be bust. Typical of the Conservatives, selling busted goods.'

'What d'you expect for twenty pence?' Terry had an uncomfortable feeling that his own father voted Conservative. He peered hopefully across to the Island but the skyline blurred and shimmered.

'Here's Rufus, hurrying — for him,' Fiona said. They watched the stocky red-headed figure coming towards them, spade over one shoulder. As he drew nearer they could see that his face was as red as his hair. 'What's up Ruf?' Fiona asked.

He leaned his spade against a rock and eased the battered knapsack from his shoulders. 'Look what I found!' He rummaged in the bag and produced a dark-coloured bottle covered in mud and dirt.

'What is it?' Terry asked.

'A sealed onion-shaped wine. Look!'

'A what?'

'A wine bottle, sealed with the family crest! It's not the sort of thing you get on a farmhouse tip usually. It's dead old.' Rufus rubbed the dirt reverently from the front of the bottle and held it up for them to see. It was roughly the shape of an onion. At the base of the neck, raised glass outlined a picture of a sheep-like animal and above the initials M.W.

'Let's see?' Terry held out his hand and Rufus passed the bottle over reluctantly. 'It's an unusual shape but it's not much of a colour.'

'It's jolly rare.'

'Is it worth a lot?' Fiona asked.

'Bound to be. Some collectors would give an arm and a leg to have this! It'll be the best thing in mine. I'm not parting with it ever!' He took the bottle back from Terry. 'I'm going to wash it.'

Fiona watched him go. 'Well, at least that's taken his mind off Dad for a bit.'

'By the way,' Rufus called over his shoulder. 'I forgot to tell you, there was a man at the farm — a man in a big black car and he was talking about you two.'

Terry's heart sank. Mr Fells had a big black BMW. They ran after Rufus and caught him up. 'What did he say?' Fiona asked.

Rufus frowned in concentration. 'I didn't take much notice at first, but when this man mentioned a donkey I started listening. He said, "Two perishin' kids. Who'd have thought they'd have the nerve to take him to the Island." Then he mentioned something about a Mr Tucker having to go out there to do the job.'

Terry groaned. 'That's the man — you know — the knackersyard man.'

'Oh, curses and double curses!' Fiona banged her forehead with her clenched fist. 'It's the one thing we never thought of! And I thought we'd been so clever.'

'He wouldn't, would he?' Terry said, horrified. 'Not go out to the Island? Surely it wouldn't be allowed?'

'I don't know.' Fiona looked wretched. 'Thanks for telling us, Ruf. Come on, Terry. We've got to *do* something.' And she marched off towards town, her hair swinging like a red banner.

Terry ran after her. 'Where are we going? What *can* we do?'

'I'm going to see him,' Fiona said fiercely. 'I'm going to ... oh, I don't know, explain. Ask him to give us just a bit of time to find Zebedee a new home.'

73

'He lives the other side of town but I'm not sure of the address.'

'We'll look him up in the phone-book,' Fiona said grimly.

The first two telephone boxes didn't have any books and the third didn't even have a phone. By this time they'd reached town, so they went to the main Post Office, dodging holiday-makers with dozens of little kids that littered the pavements.

'Fells, Fells, what's his first name Terry?' Fiona leafed through the thin pages.

'John, I think. At least my Dad calls him Jack — that means John, doesn't it?'

'J. Fells . . . lucky his name isn't Brown, hey? There's only three here under "J". 15 Sycamore Drive, 2 The Crescent and "Treetops", Coppiceland. Any of those ring a bell?'

'No. I'm a prat. We've got his phone-number at home. We usually keep an eye on Zebedee in bad weather. We ought to have gone straight to my house and rung him up.'

'We could try ringing these three, but I haven't any money, have you?'

'No, 'fraid not.'

'Anyway, I'd rather see him face to face. It'd be too easy for him to put the phone down.' She helped herself to a savings form and wrote the three addresses on the back.

'D'you know where any of these are?'

'Sycamore Drive isn't far away, and The Crescent is about ten minutes' walk from here, but the last one could be anywhere. Coppiceland is a whole district.'

'Bet that's the one if it's the farthest away. It sounds right, but we'd better try them all to be on the safe side.'

'There might be a bus — but as we haven't any money that doesn't help.'

'I've got a blister starting too,' Fiona said gloomily. 'These trainers aren't as comfortable as I thought.'

The first house wasn't too far away. 'Sycamore Drive and not a sycamore in sight,' Terry said, looking at the numbers on the gates.

'Doesn't look very promising.' Fiona stopped at number fifteen. 'Just doesn't look the kind of house where people might own a donkey.'

She knocked loudly and the door opened. 'Does Mr John Fells live here?' she asked the flat-faced girl standing in the doorway.

'Uh? My dad's Mr Fells but his name is James.' Her voice, like her face, was flat and expressionless.

'Has he got a donkey called Zebedee?' Terry asked urgently.

'This some kind of a joke?'

'Come on, we're wasting time,' Fiona said. 'Sorry to bother you.' They ran, leaving the flat girl staring after them with her mouth open.

By the time they reached The Crescent fifteen minutes later, Fiona was limping. 'I'll have to cut a hole in this shoe when I get home.' She stopped to rub her sore foot. 'I'm sure they fitted me yesterday, my feet must have grown overnight.'

They found number two and plodded up the drive. It looked very quiet. They knocked, waited and then knocked again more loudly. The house remained silent.

'No one in,' Terry said, and they trailed back down the path.

'What shall we do now? We've just wasted an awful lot of time.' Fiona bent down to loosen her lace. 'We'd better try the last one.'

Just then the disembodied head of a little old man popped up over the hedge beside them. Fiona jumped.

'They're out!' the old man shouted loudly.

'Yes, we know,' Fiona said.

'Eh? I'm deaf, I can't hear you,' he yelled.

'Oh, come on,' Terry said, anxious to escape and find the third house on their list.

'We know!' Fiona shouted at the man.

'Went on holiday last week!' he shouted louder than ever.

'Thank you.' She waved and smiled as they hurried away.

'I wouldn't care to have him for a neighbour, telling the world that the house is empty. We might have been thieves.'

'We are. We stole a donkey,' she grinned.

'Anyway, that can't be the right house if they've been away all the week.'

'That just leaves "Treetops" unless he's one of those mad people who are called Jack but put themselves in the phone-book under Walter or something. How far away is Coppiceland?'

'About a mile.'

'In that case I'm taking my shoes off before this blister gets any worse.'

She sat on the pavement and removed her trainers and tied them around her neck like football boots. They trudged on.

'Well, we're in Coppiceland but I've no idea where to start looking for "Treetops",' Terry said hopelessly, looking up and down the tree-lined avenue.

'"The Moorings", "Harbour View", "Holly House",' Fiona read from the gateposts as they walked. A milkfloat came rattling past, shattering the suburban calm. Fiona leapt into the street waving her arms and the driver slowed down and stopped.

'S'cuse me, can you tell me where a house called "Treetops" is?' she called.

'I know it. I'm going past myself on the way to the depot. It's about a mile away.'

They climbed thankfully onto the wagon and as they clattered along, the obliging milkman told them all about his corns and how he suffered. 'There you go,' he said after a few minutes, crashing to a noisy halt and pointing to a huge house on the cliff top.

'Shine a light!' Terry gasped. 'It's mega-normous.'

'Lovely people though. Deliver there every day I do. Bloke called Mr Fells. Regular gent.'

'D'you know if he owns a donkey called Zebedee?' Fiona asked.

'Dunno about that but he runs a car called B-M-W. Bit faster than a donkey it is . . . tarra.' He drove away chuckling at his own wit.

They stood looking at each other and then at the impressive wrought iron gates and the beautiful grounds beyond.

'What on earth shall we say?' Terry asked.

'We'll just tell him the truth and ask him if we can keep Zebedee on the Island until September, while we look for a new home for him.'

She set off determinedly up the long drive without even stopping to put her shoes back on. Terry followed less eagerly. 'Back or front?' Fiona asked when they reached the house and stood gazing at the circular lawn, sprinklers glinting in the sun.

'Back,' Terry said, without moving.

'They've got more than enough grass here to keep him,' Fiona said, looking at the green velvet dotted with stone sculptures.

77

'Imagine the mess he'd make of it. Come on, let's get it over with.'

But before they could move, a huge Great Dane bounded around the corner of the house. One moment she was standing next to him and the next she was flying backwards, the dog's paws against her chest.

'Fiona! Are you hurt?'

She was stretched full length on her back on the gravel!

A Small Victory

'Get off!' Fiona spluttered as the huge beast began to lick her face, one large paw on either side of her head. 'Get off! My laces are choking me, you great fool!'

Terry yanked at the massive leather collar but it was like trying to uproot a tree all by himself.

'Major! Major! Here boy.' A light voice floated round the side of the house, and the dog abandoned the game and bounded away.

'Fossilised frogspawn! I thought my end had come!' Fiona, red in the face, scrambled to her feet, still struggling to untie the trainer laces that had tightened round her neck. 'Fancy escaping death by drowning with a donkey — just to get strangled by a dog! That's the last time I ever tie my shoes round my neck!'

'I'm so sorry. Did he hurt you?' The owner of the voice, pale and fresh in a pink dress stood before them. She stared at Terry who was helping unknot the laces and then at Fiona, dusty and barefooted. 'Oh dear . . . you do look . . . did you want something?'

'We've come to see Mr Fells,' Terry said. 'Mr John Fells, that is if he's the Mr Fells that owns a donkey called Zebedee.'

'Oh, then you must be . . .'

'Yes, we are.' Fiona finally got her shoes free and stared defiantly at the immaculate woman. The dog, Major, sat and licked the woman's hand with a huge lolling tongue, and she patted his broad head absently.

'You know, he didn't make the decision lightly. He really does think he's doing the best thing. Sometimes, a quick end . . .'

She's not very happy about it either, Terry thought with a glimmer of hope. He stayed silent, hoping Fiona would soft-pedal a bit. If they could get Mrs Fells on their side . . .

'You know it was us that took Zebedee to Ferryman's Island?' Fiona said.

The woman nodded. 'I think you were very brave,' she said. 'But it's no good, is it? He can't stay there all winter, it's too exposed, and there's no shelter, no water. You have to be realistic. We did try. I tried all the homes for aged horses but they were all full, and he's a queer old boy, a loner, like some people. He would have to be kept on his own. Even when he was young he never got on with other donkeys. He couldn't possibly be put in with a lot of others, he might get kicked.' She seemed to be working at convincing herself as much as them.

'Is your husband in?' Fiona asked.

She shook her head. 'He's out making . . . arrangements. He doesn't like it any more than I do but he's a realist. You've already caused him a great deal of trouble.'

'Sorry,' Terry shuffled his feet in the gravel. It seemed odd that this woman who had every right to be mad with them both, seemed to be almost pleading. But Fiona said stubbornly.

'We'd still like to speak to him. Just a couple of weeks, that's all we need. To try to find somewhere else for him to live.'

'We've got everything worked out — delivering

water and everything. Zebedee is ever so happy,' Terry pleaded.

'My husband will be back later this afternoon. I promise you nothing will happen today. Look, I'll tell him what you've just told me and ask him to phone you tonight. If you *can* find somewhere, well, he's a busy man and this business has upset him a lot, but he's very fair and if Zebedee can enjoy a few more years, well, it's up to you.'

They thanked her and left. The sun shone on the bright weed-free borders and curved paths. Under a willow tree a stone nymph stood on a pedestal. It was all very peaceful. As they pulled the perfectly oiled gates shut behind them, Fiona pointed up at the top of the house. 'Look,' she said. 'No wonder it didn't take him very long to find out where Zebedee was.'

Terry's gaze followed her pointing finger. Outlined against the blue sky was a glassed-in observatory.

'He must be able to see right across town from there,' Terry said. 'I bet he's got a telescope.'

'All that trouble we went through and we might just as well have sent him a postcard with Zeb's new address on.'

'You've got to laugh, haven't you?'

'Or cry,' Fiona said bitterly. 'If I had all their money I could put off selling one tiddly little field until Zebedee died decently of old age.'

They started for home. 'I wonder why people with loads of cash always seem to need more,' Terry pondered as they walked.

'Just the way they're made I suppose.'

'P'raps the more things you buy the more money you need to take care of them. If that's it I'm dead sure I don't want to be a solicitor or whatever my Dad's got me lined up for.'

'A solicitor! That wouldn't suit you one bit.'

'I'd rather be poor and paint pictures.'

'That's what you ought to do then. Only you'll probably be madly successful and get rich anyway. Then you can treat me to a new pair of shoes every year in memory of a fellow thief.'

Terry, feeling guilty because he was wearing comfortable trainers, glanced anxiously at her bare feet, wondering if she was going to walk all the way home without shoes.

He looked at his watch, trying to work out how far they had to go, and then stopped dead in his tracks. 'Gran!' he yelled, 'I forgot! It's half past three and visiting is over by four. Oh God – no!'

Hospital Visit

They stood looking at each other miserably. 'My mother will think I've copped out,' Terry said.

'How far from here is the hospital? Couldn't we go straight there?'

'I suppose so, only . . .' but Terry hardly liked to explain how his mother would have fussed about clean shirts and polished shoes. 'Come on,' he said. 'Let's see if they'll let us in.'

They hurried on through the centre of town. 'Quarter to four,' he said as they puffed through the hospital gates. 'I hope we're in time.'

The hospital was filled with a humming kind of quiet. A few visitors were already leaving. They found the right ward and Terry knocked timidly on a door marked SISTER.

'I'll wait here in case you need me,' Fiona said, sitting on a windowsill in the corridor and pulling on her trainers.

'Can I see Mrs Cartwright?' he asked the blue-uniformed nurse who answered his knock. She gave him a bright smile. 'She's in one of the side wards, I think her other visitor has left.'

'That was my mother.' He followed her blue-and-white back down the corridor, trying to smooth down his damp hair. The nurse pushed open a door. The room was empty except for the figure in the bed.

Terry tiptoed forward. 'Gran? It's me, Terry.' There was no movement from the bed. His heart was beating far too loudly. He stood staring down at the face that was, and wasn't, his Gran. Her eyes were open but her face was blank, one side slightly drawn down, giving her face an uncharacteristically grim expression.

Her eyelids fluttered but she did not turn her head to look at him. Terry swallowed. 'Gran?' But it was as if the person behind the face had gone away. He stood, irresolute, the awful feeling of anti-climax slowing down his heartbeat. After a bit he rested a grubby hand on her cheek. It felt reassuringly warm, but the pinkness of his skin contrasted with the grey pallor of hers. There was an empty chair by the side of the bed so he sat down. Should he speak? He didn't know what to say, or whether she would be able to hear him if he did.

'Remember Zebedee, Gran?' he tried, but his voice sounded silly in the quiet room. He sat on for a bit, thinking about Gran as she was at home in her own room, listening to all his news, jokey and bright. Suddenly he jumped to his feet. The sound of the chair scraping across the floor seemed unbearably loud yet Gran didn't stir. 'Bye Gran,' he whispered and crept out.

'All right, dear?' a nurse asked. He nodded. Back in the corridor Fiona was still sitting on the windowsill swinging her legs. She glanced at his face and said nothing as they marched silently back down the acres of polished floor and out into the sun.

'She didn't say anything,' Terry said after a while. 'But she wasn't asleep.'

'Are you coming to see her again?'

'I don't know. I think so. Yes. I'll come the days

84

my mother can't. It can't be much fun for her — just sitting there.' The town hall clock struck four-fifteen as they passed.

'I'm starving,' Fiona said. 'Want to come back to my house for eats?'

'Could I? Thanks. I'm up to my ears in trouble now with my mother so I may as well face her on a full stomach.'

The twins were back and obviously on speaking terms again.

'Did you deliver the water, Larry? Was Zebedee all right?'

'Yes I did and yes he was. Hello, what's this, I thought. Are they preparing me for shipwreck or could I be on the "Donkey Delivery Run"? Anyway, I topped up his tank and pulled his ears for him.'

'Does he look okay?' Terry asked eagerly.

'Fine and dandy. Have you two been rumbled yet? Rufus said something.'

''Fraid so.' Fiona sprinkled oil and vinegar on the salad she was making. 'But we've got a couple of weeks to try to find him a new home. We went and saw the owner's wife. She was quite decent really.'

'Well, best of luck. He's a nice old moke. P'raps he'll start eating seaweed and live for ever.'

'What time will Liza be back from London?' Rufus asked.

'I told you twice already, Ruf. Late. Last train probably.' Larry took a couple of apples from a dish, then lifting the charts from the bookshelf unrolled them on the floor in front of the fireplace.

Josh picked out a couple of soaring notes on his flute then jotted something down in a notebook.

'D'you think *she'll* want to tell Ma about Dad's accident?' Rufus persisted.

85

'Dunno,' Larry said absently, poring over his calculations.

Josh said, 'We'll ring Saudi tomorrow Ruf, and find out exactly how Dad is, don't worry.'

Terry and Fiona ate at the cluttered table, finishing their meal with cheese and figs and a strong ginger beer that Liza made in a large vat in the pantry.

'I'd better be off.' Terry was reluctant to leave the busy cluttered cottage and face his mother. 'I should have phoned my ma from the hospital and reversed the charges, but that would have brought her out in a rash.' He pushed his chair back and Fiona followed him to the door. 'Bye everyone. Thanks for the meal. I hope the news about your dad is good tomorrow.'

'And your Gran. I'll see you tomorrow to find out what Mr Fells has to say on the phone tonight,' Fiona called after him.

'*If* he bothers to ring.'

He walked home slowly, feeling shut out. When there was trouble a family closed ranks, but in *his* family he had been excluded as well, from Gran's illness. Or was he? Hadn't he deliberately not wanted to know? He could have insisted on seeing Gran ages ago. When he reached home he managed to explain first.

'Sorry I'm late. I've been to see Gran.'

'Terry you didn't! Not looking like that! Honestly, I don't know what's got into you since you met that girl.'

'Gran never looked at me anyway.'

His mother softened. 'I know love. I left myself at half past three. There just didn't seem any point in just sitting there.' She sighed and got up. 'You'd better have this dinner, though I'm warning you it's all dried up.'

86

He was sitting pushing the dried-up dinner down his reluctant throat to avoid further argument when his mother nearly choked him by saying suddenly, 'Terry, did you know Zebedee was gone?'

'Er, what? Yes.'

'I'm awfully sorry dear.'

He stared at her. She obviously didn't know anything about Zeb being on the Island. So Mr Fells hadn't been in touch. She must think he'd already been destroyed.

'It hasn't been much of a summer for you so far, has it?'

'Oh, I don't know.' He wriggled uncomfortably in his seat. 'I think I'll do some sketching.' Escaping upstairs to fetch his things, he settled as close to the phone as he could. Absorbed, drawing from memory the Great Dane in its 'Gracious Living' setting, he used the contrast of Fiona in her shabby gear sprawling on the gravel. It was a complicated picture to compose from memory and the pile of scrap grew rapidly. When the phone rang he jumped visibly and snatched it up.

Mr Fells said, 'Is that you, young man?'

'Er, yes.' His mother was crossing the room assuming the call was for her. Terry put his hand over the mouthpiece. 'It's for me, Mum.'

'I understand from my wife that you and your girlfriend have now admitted removing my donkey from his field without permission.' He sounded grim.

'Er, yes.' His mother was staring at him and he felt his face going red. He hardly ever had any phone calls, Fiona not being on the phone and no one else ever ringing him.

'Well young man, you have two weeks to find

a completely suitable new home. In the meantime you must care for Zebedee properly and see that he has enough fresh water and comes to no harm. Understand?'

'Understood,' Terry echoed.

'As you know, he can't possibly remain on Ferryman's Island beyond early September and the next low tides, so if you aren't successful by then you and your lady partner will just have to face up to a few facts of life.'

'Thank you very much,' Terry muttered, wishing his mother would go away.

'Don't thank me, thank my soft-hearted wife.' Mr Fells rang off abruptly and Terry replaced the receiver with a sigh of relief.

'Who on earth was that?'

'Just a man we're doing some odd jobs for, to earn extra pocket money.'

'What kind of jobs, what man? I know I stopped your pocket money because of your broken glasses, but you don't have to . . . I suppose that poor girl gets enough to eat?' she interrupted herself.

'Oh yes. Her big sister cooks nice things. Vegetarian stuff.'

'Hmm. You must bring her to tea one day. As long as you give me a bit of warning. And the younger one. What's his name?'

'Rufus. Yes, okay, thanks.' He was glad to get away from the subject of the phone call and what odd jobs they were supposed to be doing. He tried to imagine his mother's face if he'd said, 'Just rowing out to Ferryman's Island to water a donkey.'

'The nearer you stick to the truth the better chance you have of getting away with it,' Fiona had said to him once. After all, looking after a donkey on an island was a very odd job when you come to think of it. He grinned to himself.

'What are *you* smiling about?' his mother asked.

'Nothing. Just something Fiona said today. I think I'll go up to bed and have a read.' He picked up his drawing things. 'I'm knackered.'

'Don't use that word, it's not very nice.'

'It's okay. We looked it up in the dictionary at the cottage. It just means worn out, useless, you know, like the knacker's yard where they shoot old horses.'

She gave him a funny look. 'Yes, well . . . Goodnight Terry.'

'Night Mum.'

'Oh and Terry.'

His heart sank. 'Yes?'

'I'm glad you went to see Gran.'

He relaxed. 'That's okay. I'll go again if you like. I'll take Fiona, she said she would come.' He climbed the stairs slowly. Knacker's yard. Where they shoot worn-out horses. And donkeys. That is, if they didn't take their evil gear and do it in the very place where he had taken refuge. He said out loud a much worse word than his mother suspected he knew, and then shot into his bedroom fast, in case she was listening.

A Trip to Town

Terry stepped on the cliff path the next morning and looked across the expanse of smooth water to where Ferryman's Island lay shrouded in mist. It was a rare hot day, coming like a gift in the middle of an indifferent summer. Below him lay the cottage, square, sturdy and apparently deserted. But as he watched, the back door opened and Fiona came out and started up the path towards him. He gave her a shout and a wave and began the steep descent, gym shoes slipping on the loose stones of the worn path.

'Did he ring?'

'Any news about your Dad?'

Their questions clashed and they both laughed.

'Yes he did,' Terry said. 'And we've got our two weeks, but he sounded madder than a shaved cat. Have you seen Zeb this morning?' He indicated the binoculars that she had slung around her neck. 'Is he still all right?'

'I got him lined up nicely earlier on. Want a look?' She gave him the binoculars. 'Larry mended them. Zeb was over on the left earlier on, eating his head off as usual.'

This time, when Terry put them up to his eyes he saw the Island clearly and the grey shape of the donkey zoomed into close-up, head down and jaws busy.

'He looks fine! Did Liza get back? Have you had a chance to phone up about your Dad yet?'

'She got back late last night. We're all going into town to phone later. She thinks Larry is right and Ma should be left in the dark till after the big demo, just as long as Dad is okay.'

She took the binoculars back and hung them around her neck.

'What else did Mr Fells say? Does your mother know yet?'

'No. I got to the phone first, but she was dead nosey. I headed her off with some tale about us doing odd jobs for a friend of yours. You're invited to tea by the way, so don't let me down. Play along.'

'Must I? I'm not very good at going to tea.'

'I had to say I'd ask you, to get her off the subject of odd jobs.'

'I suppose I'll have to come then,' she said ungraciously.

'Are you any good at hospital visits?'

'I don't mind going with you to see your Gran.'

'My mother and father are going today — Dad's got a day off work, but we could go tomorrow.'

'Yes, all right.'

They reached the cottage and sat on the sea wall in the hot sun. From inside the sound of Josh's voice carried clearly through the open window.

'I've given you all the money I've got. You know I'm cleaned out after buying this new flute.'

Then Larry, 'I'm beginning to think I should have gone ahead and found a job this summer instead of spending all my time on this blasted channel project. Especially now you've lost interest.'

'I haven't lost interest! I'm just able to look at things from more than one obsessive angle.'

Liza's clear tones interrupted. 'Are you two coming to the phone with me or not? I'd have thought you'd be too worried about Dad to keep up this arguing.'

She came out of the cottage looking harassed. 'Oh, there you are Fiona. Hi Terry! Are you both coming with us?'

'Yes please. I want to hear what they say, then Terry and I are chasing up those barrels you saw from the train.'

'Are we?' Terry said. Liza smiled. 'How did your interview go?' he asked.

'Very well Terry, and thanks for remembering to ask. It's more than some people did.' She went back indoors.

'She's a bit off this morning. The twins never seem to stop arguing, Larry didn't show any interest in her London trip — and she's dead worried about Dad of course.'

They all climbed into the Daisy-bus with Larry at the wheel. Rufus sat quiet and preoccupied and hardly showed any interest when Terry asked him how the new bottle had cleaned up. They drove into the town centre and crowded into one of the international phone-booths.

After a lot of messing about and false starts Liza managed to get through to someone in her father's firm. The rest of the family crowded around trying to hear what was being said. After a few minutes Liza said 'Goodbye' and put the phone down, looking relieved.

'He's all right. He had a bad knock on the head but his safety helmet took the worst of it, and he should be out of hospital in another week.'

'Great!' 'Thank heavens!' 'Smashing.' Only Rufus remained preoccupied while the others shouted their relief.

'You kids coming back with us?' Larry asked.

'No, we're going to find a barrel to replace the tank I pinched for Zebedee,' Fiona said. 'You coming with us, Ruf?'

'Yes, okay.'

'See you later then.' Liza and the twins went back towards the car park and the other three walked through the main shopping centre towards the railway station.

'There're my bottles,' Rufus said as they passed the secondhand shop called 'Bits & Bobs'. The window was filled with a motley assortment of articles. In the front the four pale green 'Codd' ginger beer bottles stood between a glass case of stuffed birds and an old-fashioned flat-iron. They peered through the glass trying to make out the price tags.

'Three pounds each!' Fiona exclaimed. 'And he only gave us four pounds for the four of them.'

'He hasn't sold them yet. Things hang about for ages in these kind of shops,' Terry pointed out.

They reached the warehouse where Liza had spotted some old wooden beer-barrels from the train window. Fiona persuaded the foreman to part with one for two pounds. 'But you'd better clear off with it quick before the boss comes back. I shouldn't really let you have it,' he said.

'Curses,' Fiona said when he'd gone. 'I was hoping to get Larry or Josh to fetch it in the Daisy-bus. Now we'll have to get it home ourselves. We'll have to roll it.'

'I hope my mum doesn't spot me,' Terry giggled as they struggled to control the unwieldy object along the pavement through the crowds.

'P'raps if she does she'll change her mind about having me to tea.'

93

'You don't *have* to come if you don't want to, but she's a jolly good cook and she won't try to make you eat meat or anything. You're invited as well if you want Ruf,' he added, and was surprised by the boy's immediate 'Yes please!'

They reached the bottom of the hill and started to climb. The barrel got heavier and heavier. Fiona was so puffed that she had to stop singing *Roll Out The Barrel* in her terrible flat treble and concentrate all her efforts on not letting it roll back down the hill. Rufus helped with silent determination. They finally reached the top and, turning the barrel on end to stop it rolling away, sat leaning against it on the grass verge.

'I'm never dressed right for going out to tea,' Fiona frowned down at her shabby jeans and the black and yellow trainers that now had holes cut out of the toes.

'She won't even notice,' Terry said, crossing his fingers. 'She'll just want to fatten you up.'

'Oh well, I could do with that.' Fiona sprang to her feet and, pushing the barrel over onto its side, balanced on top of it, strumming her ribs and singing some song about a girl called Boney Maloney who was as skinny as a stick of macaroni. Even Rufus laughed.

'Get off, you prat,' Terry said. 'You'll have it back down the hill in a minute and I couldn't push it up there again.'

She hopped off and stood leaning against it.

'I've got a great idea! Let's toss for who gets inside and rolls all the way down the hill in it.' She produced a coin from her pocket and held it out. 'Heads or tails?'

Terry looked at her anxiously. 'Won't it break?'

Rufus grinned and said nothing. Fiona rolled over and over on the grass, giggling helplessly. 'Your face, Terry! You thought I was serious!'

'Didn't,' Terry said, glad to see Rufus smiling. He realised Fiona was working hard to cheer Rufus up. 'Come on, let's get going,' he said.

It was almost as bad getting the barrel down the hill as it had been getting it up. It kept running away. But finally they reached the cottage and positioned it beneath the drainpipe where the tank had been. Fiona stood back and surveyed it with a satisfied nod.

'There. Now it can rain cats and dogs *and* Ma or Pa can come home any time they like.'

'I wish they would,' Rufus said, looking miserable again. Fiona sighed.

That afternoon they practised rowing in the calm bay, with Josh shouting instructions. Fiona had a good start and was fairly competent, but Terry found co-ordinating the two oars exasperating and exhausting. Just when he had one working smoothly, cutting through the waves at the right angle, the other would flatten itself, sending a shower of spray over the side of the boat.

Soon his hands were blistered and red. 'Try to relax,' Josh said. 'You're fighting the oars instead of feeling your way with them.'

'My right arm keeps pulling harder than my left, I can't seem to control it.'

'Everyone has one arm stronger than the other,' Josh said cheerfully. 'Just skip the odd stroke and you'll straighten out.'

Only Josh's patient encouragement and the thought that he must be able to pull his weight in an emergency made him persevere.

As they were stowing the oars and life-jackets away in the shed Terry said, 'Can you both come to tea on Wednesday? My mother will keep on and on until you do.'

'I suppose so.' Fiona put the rowlocks on a shelf and then turned and pulled a face. 'But don't expect me to get all ponced up, will you?'

It was odd seeing Fiona and Rufus sitting down at the table in his house. He couldn't relax. His mother had gone to a lot of trouble with the food — there was no meat in anything, he noticed. She kept up a bright chatter, but Terry knew she was noticing things like Fiona's hair tied back with string and Rufus's odd socks.

He was glad his father was home early, Ma on her own was a bit of a pill. She kept urging Fiona to eat up and then every time she picked up her fork, asking her another question. Fiona parried her questions neatly, not giving away anything but the bare facts about her family. To distract his mother, Terry said, 'Rufus collects bottles.'

'Bottles? What kind of bottles?' she asked, pouring iced squash into tall glasses.

Rufus said, 'All kinds, just as long as they're old. 'Specially medicine bottles. Look!' He plunged his hand into his pocket and produced a green glass-stoppered bottle. 'I haven't had a chance to wash it yet,' he added unnecessarily, as flakes of ancient mud fell onto the white table cloth.

'For heaven's sake, Rufus!' Fiona said, jerked out of her polite stiffness. 'Terry's mother doesn't want your Victorian germs all over the food!' Terry stifled a giggle at the expression on his mother's face.

'Sorry.' Rufus brushed absently at the dried mud

and spread it further around the cloth, staining the white fabric.

'It doesn't matter,' she said, obviously not meaning it.

'Let *me* see?' Terry's father held out his hand and Rufus gave him the bottle.

'I only picked it up this morning. Look at the letters on the side. ZENOBIA. It might be the firm's name, but it could be the kind of medicine, couldn't it?'

'I could probably find out for you if you'll trust me with it,' his father said. 'I play golf with the chemist who's got a lot of those old display bottles they used to put in the windows of chemist shops. They date back to his great-grandfather's time. Perhaps you'd like to come and see them some time?'

'Yes please!' Rufus helped himself to more cake. At least *he* seemed to be enjoying himself.

'I'll go and get the pudding.' Terry heaved a sigh of relief as his mother disappeared into the kitchen. Rufus began a long explanation on how to remove stains for Terry's father. Fiona pushed Terry's leg with her foot under the table. 'Stop looking so worried. You're making me nervous,' she whispered.

'Sorry. I'm scared Rufus will say something about Zeb.'

'I warned him about all the things he's not to mention, don't worry.'

Terry's mother came back in with a dish of bread-and-butter pudding and placed it in the middle of the table. 'And when will your father be home?' she asked, ladling out a large plateful.

'We're not sure.' Fiona glanced warningly at Rufus, but he was still deep in conversation.

'Your mother then? Surely she won't stay away much longer?'

Terry recognised the set of Fiona's jaw. 'I'll have some pudding please,' he said loudly.

'I thought you hated bread-and-butter pudding. There's ice-cream as well.' But she put him up a big helping, then returned to the attack.

'*When* did you say?'

'I didn't,' Fiona said mutinously.

'You must miss her.' She was like a terrier with a bone.

'Yes and no.' Fiona smiled and took up her spoon.

'I'll have some more, it's lovely,' Terry tried.

'You've still got a whole plateful, don't be greedy. *You* don't need to put on any weight.'

'It's rather nice not having to wash every day or go to bed early,' Fiona said.

'I wouldn't mind some ice-cream on mine,' he burst out. They ignored him.

'But we do have to help Liza of course. Doing the washing-up under the pump in the yard and swilling the washing in the sea.'

Terry gave up. There was no knowing what Fiona was likely to say now she'd started, and his mother was not famous for her sense of humour. She'd either take her seriously or think Fiona was being impertinent. He poked at his dish viciously. He hated bread-and-butter pudding.

His father saved the day. He and Rufus had moved on to discussing making a living from growing mushrooms and he drew Fiona into the conversation. Soon they were into ways of drying out fungi and alternative food sources and Fiona became animated and natural, as if she were at home with her own family. Terry relaxed. He was surprised how much his father seemed to know about the subject.

Later, when he got back from walking home with

98

them to the cottage, his father said, 'I like your friends Terry. I bet we hear a lot more about that girl in the future. She'll go places.'

'His mother said, 'I wonder if they'd be offended if I offered that lad some of Terry's socks?'

Fiona's Surprise

The days slid by. They went on practising in the boat. Only after hours of practice could Terry finally take the *Spinthrift* in the direction he wanted to go, without shipping too much water or wasting too much energy.

'Right. Good enough,' Josh said one day. 'Now I'll teach you about tides and currents and which landmarks to look for if you ever need to row out to the Island.'

Josh was a natural teacher, making everything clear and easy to follow and never moving on until they had understood the last point. 'He could show the staff in our school a thing or two,' Terry said as he and Fiona were hauling the boat up the beach after one of the sessions.

'It's a gift. He's been teaching me Maths since I was seven and he was thirteen. That's why I'm so far ahead.'

Terry patted the side of the boat almost lovingly. Thanks to Josh he was at home in it, moving confidently like the others. They were visiting Zebedee regularly, taking him carrots and other treats, and he looked healthier and younger every time they saw him.

'Liza rang Saudi again yesterday,' Fiona said. 'Dad's getting better though he still hasn't written himself.'

'Does Rufus still want Liza to tell your mother?'

'I think so, but all the rest of us have decided to wait until after the big demo.'

Coming with me to see Gran this afternoon?' She nodded. They visited Gran regularly now. She still hadn't spoken, but sometimes the faded blue eyes stared at them as if trying to puzzle out who they were.

On their first visit together, they had sat either side of the bed, talking in whispers — mainly about Zebedee and their failure to find him a suitable home. They had written to ten addresses collected from *Horse & Hound, Animal World,* and other magazines, but the replies said they had no places for a lone donkey. Most of them had long waiting lists, and so far they had spent two pounds twenty-four pence on postage without a single result.

Mr Fells had said two weeks, and soon the time had come to return to the big house in Coppiceland. This time Mr Fells was in and he asked them into the house where they sat perched on a cold, brown leather sofa, and Fiona tried to hide her dirty big toes under the edge of an oriental rug. Mr Fells had seemed slightly more friendly.

'We visit Zebedee regularly and he's looking ever so well,' Terry assured him.

'I know lad.' Mr Fells, who had obviously done his homework, knew the exact date for getting Zebedee off the Island. Terry wondered whether he actually visited him or just kept watch from his observatory, but didn't like to ask. Certainly they never saw a sign of him whenever they were there.

'No luck with the refuge homes?' They shook their heads miserably. 'Well, keep trying. Since you're looking after him so well you can have a couple of extra weeks.'

They had left for home feeling relieved and worried at the same time.

At first, discussing these and other problems across Gran's flat white bed, they had felt awkward — talking in front of someone who may, or may not, have been listening. So after a while they began to include her in their conversation.

'See Gran, we had to do something quickly. It was no good asking first and being told to mind our own business, was it?

Fiona always talked as though Gran could hear and understand. 'After all, you never know and it would be awful if she *was* lying there listening all the time and feeling left out,' she said as they walked home from the hospital one day.

So, gradually, they told her the whole story. How they had crept out at night and led Zebedee across the causeway, and about the field being auctioned. Sneaking into the back of the crowded room at the Royal Oak to hear Zebedee's old home being knocked down for a staggering £43,000 to a local builder.

After a while it stopped being odd, talking to someone who gave no sign whether she heard them. She was just there — Gran, listening like she'd always been.

On the days when Terry went on his own, he sat chatting to her in a one-sided conversation. He told her how he'd chosen four of his best Zebedee drawings and stuck them neatly into a hessian-covered square of hardboard and given it to Fiona for her thirteenth birthday.

'She was dead pleased Gran, I could tell, even though she didn't say much. She hadn't even let on it was her birthday — Liza did — so it was a good surprise. Mind you, it was a bit weird, giving some of my pictures away. Like giving away a bit of myself. D'you think Grampa felt like that?'

It was easy telling Gran things like this. Things he couldn't tell his mother. Walking back to the bus-stop that day, he thought about the odd thing that had happened a few days after Fiona's birthday. She had asked him if the pictures were hers to do as she liked with? As if he was likely to ask for them back!

'Of course, they're yours,' he told her. 'They're your birthday present.'

He'd sneaked a look at her bedroom walls next time he was at the cottage, expecting to see them hung, but they hadn't been there. His artist's eye had pictured them, bold against the whitewash, and he'd been hurt to discover there was no sign of them hung anywhere in the cottage.

Then, a couple of days later, he and Fiona were walking through town to the hospital, when she pulled his arm. 'Terry, I've got something to show you.'

She led him up the Town Hall steps and along a corridor, past posters advertising the town's Festival Week. He noticed ART EXHIBITION on the door of the room and then they were inside.

There were pictures everywhere, covering walls and display screens. Fiona walked unhesitatingly to the wall at the far end and stood looking, not at the wall, but at Terry's face.

There, straight in front of him, were the sketches of Zebedee that he had given her for her birthday. His name and age were printed clearly at the bottom, and a blue card stating FIRST PRIZE was pinned above.

Terry looked and looked without speaking. His

eyes took in the second prize-winner — a collection of sketches of people in sporting activities. Strong, powerful lines, a tennis player, a skater. Then third prize: five sketches of birds in flight. They were good. His gaze returned to his own drawings. But his were better. His had been placed first!

'Blimey!' he said at last.

'You don't mind, do you?' Fiona sounded pleading.

Did he? He didn't know. He went on, silently staring. Then he said, 'First! Just wait till old Carey hears about this!'

'It's a special class, for collections of up to six action shots in pencil or crayon. They were so good I wanted everyone to see them, so I filled in an entry form in your name. You did say they were mine to do as I liked with. You've won fifty pounds.'

'Fifty quid! We can use it to keep Zebedee somewhere like the Riding School while we look for a field.'

She grinned. 'That did cross my mind, but it's your money. You aren't mad then, about me entering the drawings?'

Before he could reply a man and woman paused beside them and studied the drawings. 'Now they *are* good,' the woman said, pointing to the Zebedee board.

'A worthy winner,' the man agreed.

Terry felt a warm glow. 'No, I don't mind,' he said.

Fiona sighed with relief. 'Liza said I should have asked you first but I was afraid if I told you, you might not enter.'

'Probably wouldn't have. I never think they're good enough.'

104

'That's why you'll get better and better. Well, we'd better get going or visiting will be over.'

Terry was reluctant to tear himself away from the pictures. He would have liked to stay and listen to any other comments people might make. 'We'll tell Gran all about it,' he said.

When they reached the hospital the Sister stopped them. 'Mrs Cartwright has been moved to the main ward, dear. We're hoping a bit more noise might stimulate her now that her condition has stabilised.'

'What does she mean — stabilised?' Terry whispered as they walked down the corridor to the main ward.

'I think it means she's staying the same. Not getting any worse.'

Indeed, Gran turned her head slightly, seeming to look right at them as they came around the curtains shielding her bed. They pulled up two stools and sat by the bed. Gran gave them a small smile.

'Gran, you're better!' Terry said.

The frail head gave a tiny nod. They talked to her quietly, telling her about the competition and though she didn't speak, her eyes followed their faces and she seemed to understand.

'I only hope Mum lets me spend the money how I like,' Terry finished, 'even if it does mean I'll have to let on about Zebedee.'

'They're bound to be pleased about you winning a prize. Parents always are,' Fiona said.

'I expect so, though I don't think Dad reckons much on drawing as a hobby.'

The bell rang then for the end of visiting, and they stood up to go. 'Bye Gran. We'll come again the day after tomorrow.' Her hand moved slightly, and Terry leaned closer.

'Terry,' she said, quite clearly.

'Yes Gran?'

There was a pause, then she said, 'Keep it up, the donkey rescue.' Quite clearly.

'We will Gran, don't you worry.' They both gave her a kiss on her thin dry cheek and waved when they reached the door. Gran gave the ghost of her old smile. Terry swallowed a lump in his throat. 'At last. She's getting better.'

More Bad News

Terry woke the next day feeling great. Gran was getting better, his drawings had won first prize in a big art competition. Perhaps the third good thing to happen would be finding a permanent home for Zebedee.

In less than two weeks they would be back in school, and soon after that the autumn low tides would occur. Time was literally running out with the tide. He jumped quickly from the bed. He'd call for Fiona early and they would think of a new approach. Surely with fifty pounds to spend they could at least find somewhere to take him temporarily when he left the Island?

His mother and father, pleased with his news about the prize, were planning to visit the exhibition themselves. His mother would visit Gran that afternoon. She had been thrilled, too, by the news of Gran speaking, though inclined to keep asking, 'Are you *sure* you didn't imagine it?' But once she had rung Sister and had it confirmed, she couldn't wait to see the improvement herself. Perhaps, Terry thought, now would be a good moment to tell her all about Zebedee.

But when he went down for breakfast, he found his mother in one of her fussy moods, not able to sit still for five seconds. Before he could broach the subject she was off upstairs hoovering Gran's room 'just in case'. In the end he decided to put off telling her until he'd discussed it with Fiona.

Then, just as he was about to leave the house, the phone rang.

'Terry, it's for you!' his mother called him back. His heart knocked guiltily. What if it was Mr Fells to say their time had run out? But his mother, handing him the receiver, said, 'It's a reporter from the local paper. He wants to talk to you about your winning entry.'

His mother stood, glowing with pride, listening to his end of the conversation.

Yes, he'd always drawn, ever since he could remember.

No. He'd never before entered a competition.

Yes, Zebedee was a real donkey.

He missed the next bit, glancing anxiously at his mother, wishing she would go away, dreading the reporter's next question. They wanted a picture of him. Could they call with a photographer the following afternoon? Anxious to get off the phone before he asked any more questions about Zebedee, Terry agreed to two o'clock. He escaped his mother's questions and set off thankfully to meet Fiona.

Rufus was mooching about outside the cottage.

'Hi Ruf. You going digging?'

'Don't know. That site is nearly exhausted. I've only got a bit of infilling left to do.'

Terry, feeling he'd neglected Rufus and the bottles lately, what with hospital visiting, taking water to Zebedee and looking for fields, said, 'I'll come and give you a hand if you like.'

'Doesn't matter.' He kicked at a pebble. 'Liza's got

another interview for that job in London. She had a letter this morning.'

'That's great!'

Rufus didn't answer.

'You don't seem very pleased. What's up?'

'It's okay for you!' Rufus burst out. 'You always know where your mum and dad are. *You* haven't got a dad with a busted head who's thousands of miles away, and a mother you can't even telephone, camping out with a load of weirdos.' He marched towards the beach, leaving Terry staring after him open-mouthed.

Terry went into the cottage feeling shaken. He had thought that Rufus agreed with the others, approving of what their mother was doing. To discover that while *he* was envying Fiona her family, Rufus was envying him *his,* took a bit of getting used to.

Inside, Liza was reading her letter aloud to the other three. She waved to him as he entered. 'Hi Terry, listen to this!' She finished the letter inviting her to attend a second interview. 'So, I'm off to London again the day after tomorrow. Isn't that great?'

'Great,' he echoed, feeling that this wasn't the moment to tell them about Rufus's outburst.

Larry said, 'There'll be other candidates with better qualifications. Don't build your hopes up.'

'Oh, pooh to that. That is *my* job. I feel it in my infallible bones. It's exactly what I've been waiting for, a new magazine with all the right ideas.'

'I've got some news as well.' Terry told them about the reporter coming the next afternoon.

'Fame at last. We'll soon be asking you for your autograph.'

When they were outside Fiona said, 'Let's go and check if there's any room now at the Riding School.

That is, if you still want to spend all your money on Zebedee.'

'I don't mind, but it's getting my hands on it without letting on what I want it for. You know what parents are like. My dad had it invested in a building society before I could see the colour of the ink.'

'Let's go and look for fields then. I checked the map again last night and listed all the farms we haven't called on yet.'

They went to the stables first, but the owner said they were still full up, and with the autumn coming on they were too short of pasture to take any grass livery.

'Let's see if Rufus is back. P'raps he'd like to come with us and look for new bottle sites. He's been dead narky lately,' Fiona said. But when they reached the cottage there was a shabby green van parked outside and inside the cottage a woman was sitting at the table talking to Liza and the twins. They slipped in and stood quietly by the door until Liza noticed them.

'This is my sister Fiona and her friend Terry. This is Fay Donovan,' she introduced them. 'She's come with news about mother.'

'What about mother? Fiona asked sharply.

'It's all right, dear. Last night there was a protest demo and she and another woman cut the wire into the camp and they were involved in an incident.'

'What does that mean?' Fiona asked.

'They lay down in front of the trucks that were carrying missiles. Your mother is a very brave woman.'

What's happened to her?'

'She's being questioned at the moment. The Military Police are keeping the Press out of it. They don't like us to get publicity.'

'You mean she's been arrested?' Fiona asked.

Fay Donovan nodded. 'She asked me to come and explain to you until she can write herself . . .' There was a sharp exclamation from the doorway. Rufus had come back without them noticing.

'What's happened to my mother? Why hasn't she come back?' He rushed at the woman and grabbed her arm, his face red and furious.

'Steady on, Ruf, old chap,' Josh said.

'I was just explaining dear . . .'

'Rufus! Where are your manners?' Liza sounded just like Terry's mother. 'Mrs Donovan has been kind enough to travel down especially to tell us. Nothing terrible has happened. Ma will just be fined or something . . .' She looked to Fay Donovan for support and the woman nodded encouragingly.

'How do *you* know?' Rufus turned his anger on Liza. 'They put them in prison sometimes, I've seen it in the papers. What do *you* care anyway? All you're interested in is your rotten old job in London. You don't care about Dad or Ma or anyone!' He turned and bolted from the room, out into the garden.

Josh started after him but Liza said, 'Best let him cool off. I'll have a talk with him then and explain things properly. He's probably imagining all kinds of things.'

Terry and Fiona helped with lunch and Fay stayed to eat with them. None of them enjoyed the meal much. Terry wondered if he should mention Rufus's earlier outburst, but there didn't seem much point.

Larry, Josh and Liza questioned Fay about the recent events in the Peace Camp. 'What can we do to help Ma?' Josh asked.

'Sit tight for a day or so and see if the police press charges. And keep your appointment Liza, for the London job. Your mother would hate you to miss that.'

'What about Dad though? She still doesn't know about his accident. Thank goodness he's getting better. I phoned again yesterday and there's a letter from him on its way.'

'I think your mother would want to know any news about the family — good or bad. I'll take a letter from you if you like.'

'Good idea,' Larry said. 'Let's all write a round-robin.' He went to fetch paper and pens.

'Are you going straight back to the camp?' Fiona asked.

'No, I'm calling on the family of the woman who was arrested with your mother. I'm spending the night with them before driving back to the camp tomorrow.'

Fiona wrote her scribbled paragraph, and then went over to Terry. 'Let's go and see if we can find Rufus.'

They went outside and gazed across the deserted beach.

'As if we haven't got enough to worry about without Rufus acting up,' she said crossly.

'He's awfully miserable,' Terry protested.

'Who isn't?' Fiona set off across the beach. Terry followed. She must be worried sick about her mother, he thought. He'd never known anyone who had been arrested before. Not that he actually *knew* Fiona's mother, but it still gave him a queer feeling. What would his own parents think if it got into the papers? He made up his mind to defend her whatever his mother said.

They stopped and looked out at the blank empty sea. It went on lapping at their feet indifferently.

Someone shouted behind them and they turned to see Larry crossing the shingle. 'He looks grim,' Fiona said, starting back towards him.

Larry waved a piece of paper at them, 'Silly little mutt has run away.'

'What! How d'you know?'

'He left this note under a stone on the gatepost. It says he's gone to Brownlea to the Peace Camp to try to see Ma.'

Back at the cottage, Liza studied the note. 'GONE TO SEE MA. DON'T WORRY. RUFUS.'

'He can't have got far, he hasn't got any money,' Josh said. 'Pity Fay left before we found this, she could have looked out for him along the road.'

'He'd never hitch-hike after all the times he's been told how dangerous it is ... would he?' Liza said, looking white and strained.

'We'll take the Daisy-bus and go and look for him,' Larry said. 'Come on, Josh.'

'Shall Terry and I come?' Fiona asked.

'Someone should stay here in case he comes back. It'd better be me,' Liza said. 'I feel terrible now, stopping Josh from going after him earlier.'

'Not your fault,' Josh said. 'Will you and Terry try the bottle site, Fiona?'

But the farmyard was deserted, the site neatly sectioned with string, almost completely filled in. They walked back home, arriving at the same time as the twins. Josh gave a thumbs-down sign.

'Hop in, we're going to check the bus and rail stations in case he's got some money,' Larry said.

In town he dropped Terry and Fiona off at the railway station while he looked for somewhere to park. 'I'll pick you up here in twenty minutes when I've covered the bus station,' he said as he drove away.

Inside the station a man told them a train had left for Brownlea an hour before, but he couldn't remember a red-haired boy about nine buying a ticket. 'Are you sure?' Fiona insisted, while the queue behind shifted restlessly.

'Might have, might not,' the porter said irritatingly.

'How much would it be?' she asked. He looked at a chart.

'Half-fare would be twelve pound thirty pence and he'd have to change twice.'

'He wouldn't be able to afford that,' Fiona said as they went back outside to wait for Larry and Josh. 'Unless . . .'

'Unless he's sold his Onion Seal,' Terry finished.

'Come on. We've still got fifteen minutes.' She grabbed his hand and they ran through the crowded pavements to 'Bits & Bobs'.

Mr Bob was outside, polishing his brass letterbox lovingly. 'Hello, young lady. Come to buy or sell?'

'Neither. We're looking for my brother, Rufus. Have you seen him today?'

'Not today.'

'When then, recently? Did he sell you any bottles?'

'Transactions are private,' Mr Bob said, huffing on the brass.

'It's very important that we know.'

'Why? Didn't he give you your cut?' he grinned at her.

'Mr Bob, can you keep secrets?'

'Better than most. Why?'

'Because Rufus is in trouble. He's run away. We need to know how much money he might have. We don't care which bottles he sold, they were all his to sell.'

114

Mr Bob stopped grinning. 'I did buy a good Onion Seal off him three days ago.'

'Three days ago!' Terry said. 'Then he must have been planning something. He loved that bottle.'

'I played fair. Told him I was no expert and he ought to take it to London and get it valued properly, but he said if I didn't want it, he was offering it to "Nic-Nacs" over the road.'

'How much?' Fiona asked.

Mr Bob looked pained. 'He wouldn't have got a fiver off that shyster in "Nic-Nacs", but I gave him twenty pounds . . .'

'Thanks Mr Bob, that's what we need to know. 'Bye.'

'Let me know when you find him. He's a nice lad.'

They ran back to the station and climbed into the waiting Daisy-bus. 'He's got twenty quid. He sold his best bottle to Mr Bob three days ago,' Fiona puffed.

'He must have had some plan up his sleeve for days then. He wouldn't have parted with that bottle easily.' Larry put the old bus into gear.

They went and reported what they'd found out to Liza.

'Then at least he's on the train or bus.' Liza looked relieved. 'Not hitching. I didn't think he would, after the times he's been warned.'

'What do we do now?' Larry said. 'Inform the police and ask them to look out for him that end?'

'The Press will love that if they get hold of it,' Liza said. 'Can't you just see the headlines? "MISSING BOY IN SEARCH FOR JAILED PEACE-MOTHER".'

'Surely all that matters is that we find him safe?' Josh said.

'I think, the best plan would be for Josh and I to go to Brownlea and see if we can find him,' Larry said. 'Then visit Ma.'

'*I'm* not staying here, I'd go mad stuck waiting without a phone even,' Liza said.

'Nor me,' Fiona joined in. 'I want to see Ma as well.'

'But what if he comes back and finds the cottage shut up,' Larry said.

'We'll leave a note telling him to go to Terry's,' Liza said. 'That all right with you, Terry?'

'Yes, of course,' Terry said, glad to be involved.

'And if we leave the key with you, you can check every day to see if Dad's letter comes.'

'How long do you think you'll be gone then?'

'If we don't find Rufus, we'll contact the police straight away. And it'll probably be a few days before Ma's case comes up.' Liza ran her hands through her smooth hair.

'Well, if I'm out — visiting Gran or something — say it in code. Say, "The special crayons you ordered are now in stock". Something like that. Then I'll know Rufus is safe.'

'Good idea. I'll be Smith's Stationery.'

'What about money?' Josh said. 'I'm practically cleaned out. We'll need petrol and possibly money if Ma is fined.'

Larry said, 'Fay reckons there's a special fund for that.'

'I'll need at least twenty to get to London for my interview,' Liza said.

'I'll pawn my flute till we can get in touch with Dad,' Josh said, looking sick at the thought.

'You could have *my* fifty quid if I could lay my hands on it,' Terry said.

'Thanks Terry, that's a nice thought, but you need that for Zebedee,' Josh said.

'Zebedee!' Terry and Fiona stared at each other, horrified.

'I forgot all about him,' Terry said shakily. 'How will I manage?'

Problems

Never in his wildest nightmares had Terry ever imagined being left solely responsible for Zebedee. Now it hit him like a blow in the stomach how much he depended on Fiona and her family.

'We'll top up the water before we leave,' Josh said. 'And fill every container we can get hold of and take them over.'

'But how will I get there?' Terry asked.

'You'll have to get one of the pleasure boats to take you. They take people on trips round the other bay so you can probably hire one. Can you use some of your money?' Larry said.

'Yes. I'll tell Dad I need some oil-paints.'

'But whatever you do, *don't* try rowing there alone,' Josh warned. 'If you hit any snags tell your parents or Mr Fells. Anyway, we might be back in less than three days.'

Terry began to feel a bit better.

Josh went out to fix the outboard onto the *Spinthrift* and Fiona and Terry searched out and filled the water containers. No one spoke much on the way out. Terry, distracted by thoughts of what Rufus might be doing, hardly noticed the sea around them.

Zebedee trotted to meet them, anxious for company and carrots, but they had no time to waste. They unloaded the water containers, filled the tank to the brim and stored the rest by the broken wall.

The lightened craft zipped back across the fast-flowing tide and in minutes they were hauling the boat up the shingle and storing life-jackets and engine in the shed behind the cottage.

'I'll hide the key in the usual place in case he comes back, and so that you can go in to collect the post,' Larry said to Terry.

Liza was packing sleeping bags, blankets and camping gear into the back of the bus. Fiona, rolling up a sleeping bag and tying string around it, said quietly to Terry, 'Don't drag Mr Fells or your parents in if you can help it. It'll only prove we can't manage after all.'

'No, I won't.' He tried to ignore the sinking feeling in the pit of his stomach. He felt left out and abandoned amid all the excitement of packing. Finally they were ready.

'Good luck. I hope you find Rufus safe at the camp.'

''Bye Terry. We'll ring as soon as there's news.'

'Look after Zeb,' Fiona yelled.

He stood and waved till they were out of sight, then, feeling more alone than he ever had in his life, turned and made his way home.

The house was empty. It was four o'clock. It seemed much later, so much had happened. His mother would still be visiting Gran. He realised guiltily that he had hardly spared Gran a thought all day. He wished there was time to go to the hospital now, but visiting would be over till the evening. And if he went this evening he might miss a phone-call about Rufus. I'll go tomorrow as soon as the reporter has gone, he decided, feeling more cheerful.

His mother came back with the good news that Gran was very much improved and looking forward to seeing him. 'She's very tired, so it would be more sensible if you both wait till tomorrow,' his mother said. He didn't tell her Fiona had gone away. She was sure to ask a lot of embarrassing questions.

He managed to answer the phone every time it rang and finally there were pips from a call-box about nine o'clock. It was Fiona.

'The pencils, sorry, crayons, are not in, sir,' she said.

'It's all right. My mother is getting some washing in, and Dad's out. You can talk.'

'We haven't found him. We've reported him missing to the police now. They're being ever so nice.'

'Wasn't he on that train? Have you seen your mother?'

'No, he wasn't. They let us see Ma. I can't talk much longer, my money is running out. Ma's out on bail. She's phoned Dad. We're staying until . . .' The phone cut suddenly and Terry replaced the receiver and waited hopefully. But it didn't ring again.

'Who was that?' his mother asked coming in with a basket of washing.

'Fiona.' He didn't see any point in lying. 'They've gone away for a few days.'

His mother smiled. 'She's quite devoted, isn't she? Ringing you already.'

Terry scowled.

The next morning he went in search of a boat. It was hot and still. Zebedee's water supply would normally last three days and that would take him up until Friday, but with this hot weather he would drink

120

more *and* it would evaporate. He would feel much happier once he had fixed it up with a boat owner to take him over.

He made his way to the harbour, hating the look of the cottage, now completely deserted, with the *Spinthrift* pulled high up the beach and the usual splash of colour provided by the Daisy-bus missing.

He walked along the cliff path and around the headland, then past the sandy beach where the crowds gathered, and down to the marina where all the boats were moored. Then slowly round the edge of the harbour looking at the names. *Saucy Sue, Misty Morn, Stella*. There were plenty of boards displayed advertising 'Trips Round the Bay' or 'All Day Fishing Trips'. Terry hesitated, wishing Fiona were with him. He hated approaching strangers. At last he decided on *The Madcap*, a nicely painted motor-boat in blue and white. The owner, who was pottering around on board, was Terry's idea of a proper sea-captain. He was smoking a pipe, wearing a navy peaked cap and had a trim grey beard. He turned round at Terry's rather nervous 'Er, excuse me, do you give trips?' and, removing his pipe, gestured with it towards a chalked noticeboard on the side of the harbour. It said, 'MADCAP. RIDES ROUND BAY £1.50 per person'.

'I was thinking of a longer trip, as far as Ferryman's Island,' Terry said.

Well now, what are you prepared to pay to charter my vessel?' the man asked seriously.

'I don't need it yet. Not until Friday morning — if then. That is, I *might* not need it at all . . .' he floundered.

'Friday, eh? Right near the weekend. And not even a firm offer? This is getting more expensive every minute.' He replaced the pipe between his teeth, smiling.

Terry took a deep breath. 'The thing is, I may need to take water over to the Island for a donkey, or at least to visit him to top his tank up. The water is already there. But only if my friends with a boat don't get back by then.'

The man regarded him with interest. 'Oh, he's yours, is he? I wondered where he came from. He's having a high old time for himself.'

'He's not exactly mine. I'm sort of looking after him.'

'Well, if you're here dead on eight o'clock on Friday morning, I'll take you. If you don't turn up — right on time mind — I'll assume my services aren't required. That do you?'

'Oh yes, thanks. What do you charge?'

'Say a fiver? That suit?'

'Yes. Fine.' He walked home, relieved to have the matter settled, feeling happier about Zebedee, but still worrying about Rufus. He had lain awake a lot of the night before wondering wherever he could be. He must have decided to hitch after all. But he surely wouldn't have taken as long as this? Perhaps they'd found him by now. He imagined Rufus, withdrawn and silent, plodding along busy roads, worrying about his mother and father. He wished there was somewhere he could phone to find out what was happening.

When he got home he spent the rest of the morning drawing a slow-worm he found in the garden, sunning itself on a stone. Gradually getting so absorbed that he forgot everything, Rufus, Zebedee, Gran and all.

After lunch his mother said she was off to see Gran.

'Give her my love. Tell her I'll come as soon as the reporter has gone,' Terry said.

'Make sure you wash and change. Put on your best pullover,' his mother said.

'It's too hot for that.'

'Well, a clean shirt then. Your blue one with the short sleeves.'

He wished she would go and stop fussing. 'Yes, all right.' At last she left and he stood willing the phone to ring with some news. 'Oh Terry!' He jumped. His mother had come back again. 'I forgot to tell you, there was a phone-call while you were in the garden.'

'What? Why didn't you call me?'

'There wasn't time. It was rather odd. A man who said he was from Smith's Stationers ringing from a call-box. Something about the crayons you wanted not being in yet. I thought it was a practical joker. Does it make sense?'

'Yes. No. Sort of.'

'What crayons are they, then?'

'You're going to be awfully late. Gran will be worrying.'

'Yes, you're right. Goodbye dear. Change those grubby shorts as well.'

He groaned, then sighed with relief when he finally heard the Mini's engine. What exactly had Josh or Larry said? The wording was important. 'The crayons are not in yet.' So Rufus wasn't found. It occurred to Terry to look in the newspaper and see if his disappearance was mentioned. He searched through his father's *Daily Telegraph* but couldn't find anything. The doorbell rang, startling him, and he opened the door to two men. The taller one produced a card and said, 'Terry Evans? We're from the *Daily Echo*.'

The other man, small and ferrety with darting eyes, was holding a camera. He said, 'Right, where is he?'

'Where's who?' Terry asked stupidly.

'The donkey. Zebedee. I want a picture of the two of you together.' He had a spotted yellow bow-tie and pale blue suede shoes.

The tall man said, 'Hold it, Con, let's ask the lad a few questions about the competition.'

'I didn't say he was *here* when you phoned,' Terry said. 'I just said he was a real donkey.'

'Sorry lad. Wires crossed. Where is he then? Con's keen on animal shots.'

'Actually,' Terry said, caught off-guard, 'he's out on Ferryman's Island.' And immediately could have bitten off his tongue.

'What!'

'Oh, dandy.' The man with the camera pulled irritably at his bow-tie. 'How the hell are we supposed to get *there* in a Beetle wagon?'

'What's he doing on the Island?' the reporter asked. 'And how on earth did he get there?' Terry muttered something about low tides, wishing he'd kept his mouth shut. 'You mean you took him?'

'Me and a friend from school. He used to live behind this house, but his field has been sold.' Terry was no match for the reporter who was obviously hot on the scent of a 'human interest' story. The more he tried to evade his questions the keener he got. 'Like to show us this field?' he suggested.

Terry led them down the garden and across the lane to the field. 'What d'you think, Con? One of the lad standing by the estate agent's board showing the SOLD sign?'

'He could be holding a picture of the donkey. Have you got one, Terry?' Con asked, getting enthusiastic.

Terry returned to the house and fetched his largest picture of Zebedee. 'Open the gate,' Con directed. 'Sort of symbolic.' He leapt about, getting his pale shoes coated in dust as he took shots from different angles.

'Look a bit more miserable kid,' he yelled as Terry gave a nervous smile. 'And hold the picture straight. That's it!'

When they had finished they trooped back to the house and the tall reporter asked Terry a lot more questions about his painting and drawing. Then as they were leaving he returned to the subject of Zebedee and the Island. Terry, trying to keep Fiona and Mr Fells names out of it, answered cagily. He heaved a sigh of relief when they finally climbed into a bright green Beetle wagon and disappeared.

Whew, thank goodness that's over and Ma wasn't here, he thought as he washed and put on the clean clothes he'd forgotten to wear for the photographs. He looked at the clock. Nearly three o'clock. He'd have to shift if he was going to see Gran.

As he hurried down the hill to the bus-stop he wondered how much of that would be in the paper the next day and whether Fiona would be annoyed. Mr Fells was sure to be!

His spirits lifted at the thought of seeing Gran. It was a pity his mother was there, since it meant he wouldn't be able to tell her about Rufus running away. It was hard to believe there was still no news about him. Where had he slept last night?

When he reached the familiar ward he almost bumped into his mother and the Sister coming out of her office.

'Oh Terry, there you are. I just rang the house.' Her voice was shaky and her eyes red and swollen.

125

Terry's heart began to hammer loudly inside his rib cage.

'Gran? Is she all right?'

'I'm so sorry,' his mother said, as if she were to blame for something. 'She's gone, dear.'

Terry in Trouble

Terry sat in the car staring at his mother. Her nose was pink and occasionally she grated the gears. She was talking but nothing she said seemed to penetrate his brain. Gran was gone. Gone where? Now his mother was saying something about phoning Dad and arranging about a certificate. Notices for the papers. He didn't know what she was talking about. He sat silent, wishing she would be quiet and give him a chance to feel his way through the cottonwool in his head.

But it was as if she couldn't stop. Daren't. Would go on talking for ever. He followed her, still silent, into the house.

'Put the kettle on, there's a good boy, while I phone your father. Oh dear! . . .'

Automatically Terry went through the right movements. Unplug kettle. Take off lid. Fill with water. His mother's voice washed over him. She was talking on the phone now.

'Yes . . . yes . . . The end was quite peaceful. About half an hour after I reached the hospital this afternoon.'

That would be when he was having his stupid photo taken. He felt a fierce resentment that his mother had been there and he hadn't. The fact that it wasn't her fault didn't seem to count.

'She just passed on quietly in her sleep.'

Terry switched the kettle on and with the click the muzzy sensation cleared from his brain.

'She didn't pass on!' he yelled. 'She died! She's dead! Why don't you say what you mean?'

He ran. In the hall his mother stood holding the phone, her blotchy white face with its pink nose staring at him, her mouth open, but silent at last. He wanted to laugh loudly at the expression on her face.

He ran out of the house and down the cliff path, on and on, faster and faster. He was no athlete but, incredibly, he reached the cottage without falling. Its empty tidiness hit him. The windows closed, door locked. No washing draped over the lilac bush. He flung himself down on the grass. No Fiona.

Fiona would have known to keep quiet, he thought. But she too was gone. He jumped up angrily, trying to smother the thoughts whirling around in his head. He retrieved the key to the shed from its hiding place in the wall and fetched the oars and rowlocks. Then he overturned the boat and dragged it into the sea. He pushed off, jumping in at the last minute, ignoring his wet feet.

He had to do something, *anything,* to stop himself thinking about Gran. He fitted the rowlocks and oars and started to row. He needed to see Zebedee. The donkey was part of his life with Gran and Fiona and now he was the only one left.

He rowed with the same quick economy that he had admired in Josh all those weeks ago. It was as if the anger inside him had turned him into a different person, changing even the way he rowed. Each blade struck the water cleanly and powerfully. He took his siting from the Bull's Nose Rock and changed direction to use the flow of the tide, registering the

128

signs without conscious thought, using the current that would take him to the shingle beach.

The sea was glassy and calm. He didn't stop rowing until he felt the scrape of shingle under the bows. Then he shipped the oars neatly and jumped out, knee-deep in the warm swelling waves, and began hauling the *Spinthrift* up the incline. Only when the boat was safely beached did he stop, gasping, realising just what he'd achieved. He, the only kid in his class who couldn't swim. He, who had been terrified of water ever since he could remember, had rowed here alone. Just wait till he told Gran! . . .

A wave of desolation hit him. He left the boat and trudged across the rocks. Zebedee came to meet him. Terry hugged the donkey's warm brown neck. 'Hello, old friend. No carrots today. Sorry.'

He took off his glasses and buried his face in the thick hot fur. When he finally raised his head there was a large damp patch on the donkey's coat. He could never tell Gran anything, ever again.

The sun burned the back of his neck. After a while, Zebedee shifted restlessly and Terry left him and lay on the sweet-smelling grass. The donkey stayed nearby, grazing, his scrawny tail flipping away at flies, the bony head moving steadily along the grass as he chewed. Terry closed his eyes as the hot sun burned his face. The sound of waves rattling over pebbles, the crunch of the animal's jaws, seabirds calling and the smell of warm earth all mingled. After a while he slept.

The rain woke him. Cold and stinging, it jerked him into consciousness. He sat up, startled, unable to take in where he was or what had happened. Then he remembered. He scrambled to his feet. The sun had disappeared behind angry piles of purple-grey clouds on the horizon.

He looked around. The only shelter was the tumble-down, roofless hut. He ran towards it and crouched in the corner where the walls met. A streak of lightning split the sky, followed almost immediately by a sharp crack of thunder.

Terrified, Terry watched as the surrounding waves piled up, crashing against the rock of the Island as if determined to sink it. He huddled against the walls, the rain streaming down his face, soaking his shirt.

Zebedee came over and pressed close to him, seeking comfort.

'It's all right boy, it's only a storm.' But his voice trembled and was lost in the next great crash and rumble. The sky was a violent purple now and a cold wind pushed the sea about as if it were soup, stirred by a giant ladle. Even as he shivered and hugged the donkey closer, one part of Terry's mind was registering the marvel of colours. He had never before been out in a storm. His mother hated them and pulled all the curtains.

His shorts and shirt were clinging to him and his feet, already wet from the sea, were numb and cold. He buried his face in Zebedee's wet fur and prayed for it to stop. The memory of his mother's face, as she had looked when he ran past her, came back to him, white and shocked. He didn't feel like laughing now. She would be worried sick, already upset as she was about Gran. Perhaps she would think he was at the cottage? Then he remembered — she knew Fiona and her family were away.

He thought the storm would never pass, but gradually the lightning grew less frequent, and the gaps between flashes and thunder longer and longer. Then

130

a line of greeny-blue appeared on the horizon and the heavy clouds began to lift.

Shivering, Terry crawled out of his shelter and looked about. The air was damp and chill, and the sea grey and agitated. At the thought of the return trip his heart failed him. Would he have the courage to row across a sea like that? He stumbled across the slope and down the rocks, his mind as churned up as the water. Then he started to run.

The *Spinthrift* had gone!

Terry is Trapped

He stood at the edge of the sea staring across the stretch of water that separated him from the bobbing boat. How could he have been so stupid? They had trusted him not to use it. Hadn't even made him promise. What would happen to it? Where would it drift?

Miserably he made his way back to his shelter. A watery sun was making a comeback. Zebedee had returned to his grazing unconcerned. Terry sat on the driest bit of wall he could find and thought about the mess he was in.

Fiona and the others were away for a possible three days or even longer. His mother would have no idea where to look for him and the last place she would think of would be Ferryman's Island. And he was starving! He looked at his watch. Six o'clock. It seemed a lifetime since he had stood in the hospital corridor and heard the news about Gran. He was wet and cold but hopefully the sun would shine a bit longer and dry him off. Zebedee was already steaming in the returning heat. And at least he had plenty of fresh water!

He thought guiltily about his parents, upset about Gran and now worrying about him. He realised that he hadn't thought much about Gran in the last half hour and his misery increased. He took off his shirt and spread it on the wall in the sun, thinking longingly of the pullover he'd refused to wear earlier. Then he sat and thought about food. Sausage, beans and chips, fried eggs, crusty bread spread thickly with butter. Then he felt guilty again because he wasn't thinking about Gran. The sun set slowly, slipping into the sea in a pool of liquid gold light. Even in his misery he enjoyed watching it.

He put his damp shirt back on and scanned the sea hopefully for any kind of craft until it was too dark to see anything.

It was the longest night he had ever known. He huddled, chilled and stiff, by Zebedee's side. He must have dozed because from time to time he was jerked back into consciousness by weird dreams.

Mr Fells was rowing him along the road and up the hill from the cottage. He was shouting at him because he couldn't start the outboard on the *Spinthrift*. His face, huge and red, the moustache quivering, got bigger and bigger until Terry woke up shivering and remembered where he was.

He dozed again and dreamt Fiona's mother was insisting on riding Zebedee in a peace parade against nuclear missiles. He and Fiona were begging her to get off him because she was fat and heavy and the donkey was too old to be ridden. She waved a massive arm in the air and began to beat Zebedee with ropes of wooden beads as large as cannon-balls.

Every time he woke, shaking and sick, from one of these nightmares, he started thinking about his mother and how worried she must be. Then about the *Spinthrift* and how he'd let Josh and Larry down. Then Rufus. Had he been found? And if not, where was he sleeping? And jumbled up with all these other worries was Gran.

He couldn't think of a single nice thought. Even winning the competition had turned sour. It was having his photo taken that had stopped him visiting Gran for the last time.

The sea whispered and murmured all around him, sucking into rocks and lapping the rustling shingle. Birds called strange haunting cries. The smell of the wetness wove itself into his dreams.

As soon as the first band of light crept along the edge of the sky, Terry stretched his cramped limbs and stood up. It was barely light enough to see. Zebedee scrambled to his feet and shook himself. Terry hugged him. 'Thanks old matey. I would have frozen to death without you.' His voice sounded odd in the silent, cold air. He fumbled his way to where they had stacked the containers and drank some water. It tasted good.

During the night, for the first time, Terry had thought of his Gran not as *his* Gran, but as his own mother's mother. The more he thought of how she must be feeling this morning, the more wretched he felt.

Zebedee stretched one leg after the other and then curled back his upper lip in a huge early morning yawn. Then he moved off and started to graze on the wet turf. Wish *I* ate grass, Terry thought. Hunger was a sharp pain. He decided to jog right round the Island to warm himself up and work off the stiffness.

He set off at a shambling run and felt the blood returning to his feet and hands, then stopped for a breather at the highest point. The light was stronger now and he looked longingly at the mainland, so close, yet impossibly far away. The sea was still

134

choppy from the previous day's storm and he wondered if he would have had the nerve to take a boat across it even if he did have one.

Just as he was about to set off again he heard a new sound. The chug-chug of a motor-boat engine! Eagerly he scanned the horizon. Sure enough, in the middle of all the empty space, a small blue and white boat was heading straight towards the Island. He ran, shouting and waving, down the slope and towards the shingle beach.

As the boat drew nearer he saw it was the *Madcap* with the grey-bearded man at the helm and bouncing behind like a puppy on a lead was the *Spinthrift*!

'Hey there!' Terry called as the boat edged in closer. Then, 'Ahoy!' He felt this was a good word in the circumstances.

'Ahoy yourself!' the man called. 'Have you by any chance lost a boat?'

Terry waded to meet him and clung onto the side as the boat grounded. 'Am I glad to see you! I let it float away yesterday in the storm. Is it damaged? Thank you ever so much. How did you know I was here?'

The man cut his engine. 'I didn't, but I put two and two together when I found the dinghy drifting out to sea. I knew where she was from, and I remembered you and the donkey, so I thought I'd just take a look at the Island before getting on to the coastguards. What happened?'

Terry told him, not sparing himself in the telling. 'I'm supposed to be looking after Zebedee, but I took the boat without permission. I'm ever so grateful. Can you take me back?' he finished.

'That sounds like a good idea. Bet you spent a chilly night, but you don't seem to have come to any harm.'

'My mother will be worried sick. She doesn't know where I am and yesterday my Gran — her mother died . . .' he stopped, choking up, thinking how strange 'her mother' sounded.

'Fine old state she'll be in this morning. Well, *you've* had a rough time as well, and no mistake.'

'I didn't even have a chance to say goodbye to her.'

'If she knew you loved her, that's the main thing. She was a lucky lady. Now, is there anything you have to collect? You'd better get aboard.'

'Can I just fill up Zebedee's tank? I may as well since I'm here.'

'Cut along then.'

Terry tipped in water until the tank was full then gave Zebedee a last hug before joining the man in the boat. The *Madcap*'s owner put the engine in reverse and backed away from the shore, then threw Terry a life-jacket. 'Put that on. Did you come across without one?'

'Yes. I didn't think.'

'I wouldn't pull that stroke again. You mightn't be so lucky next time.'

'No, I won't.'

'You must be a fair little rower to handle that heavy boat on your own.'

'I used the currents like Josh showed me.' Terry stared at the *Spinthrift* bouncing along behind the *Madcap*. 'You did say she wasn't damaged?'

'You've lost an oar, that's about all.'

'Where can I buy one?'

'I'll look one out for you, I gather you're in a hurry to replace it before your friends come back?'

'I can pay. And for picking me up. I've got lots of money.'

The man laughed. 'Have you now? Perhaps I'm going about this the wrong way. P'raps I ought to claim salvage. I could you know, under the law.'

'I've got fifty pounds that I won in a drawing competition. Would that be enough?'

'Go on with you. Keep your money. You can pay for the oar. Leave the other one with me and I'll try and match it up. Come over later — if your mother lets you out!'

He dropped Terry on the beach and helped him pull the *Spinthrift* high up the shingle above the tideline and fix the anchor ropes. Terry waved goodbye, then put the rowlocks safely in the shed. He stood for a moment staring out at the Island, hardly able to believe that he'd spent the night there. Then he turned towards the hill and home, to take whatever was coming to him.

Back Home

There was no sign of anyone around the house. His father's car was missing from the drive but his mother's Mini was there. Terry let himself quietly in the back door and went through the kitchen into the living-room. His mother was sitting, staring at a newspaper on her lap.

'Mum?'

'Terry !' She stared at him as if unable to believe he was real.

'Im sorry Mum, I . . .' The next moment she was out of her chair and he was being hugged and cried over. The more he tried to explain, the more questions she asked without waiting for any answers. At last he managed to tell her he was starving and that got her into the kitchen.

The smell of the frying bacon nearly drove him mad. While he wolfed down the food, she sat opposite, firing questions at him which he could hardly answer because his mouth was full. At last, when she had heard the whole story, she fell silent except for an occasional, 'I can't believe it!' Then suddenly she jumped up, 'Your father! The police!' and ran to the telephone.

'Did you report me missing to the police?' Terry asked, when she got back.

'Certainly I did! When you went dashing off I

thought you'd want to tell Fiona about Gran, then I remembered you'd said they were away for a few days. I left it a couple of hours and then this storm started. When your father came home we walked down to their cottage just in case you were there.'

Terry mopped up his fried egg with bread. 'Any more fried bread? What did you do then?'

'The cottage was all in darkness. We looked around, not sure what to do next when we found the note?'

'What note?'

'The note in a plastic folder under a stone by the back door.'

'Oh, that one.'

'You knew about it then?'

'Yes, of course. Liza left it for Rufus in case he came back. I can't believe he hasn't been found. Where can he be?'

'His poor mother must be nearly out of her mind. I know how I felt all last night and he's been gone for *two* nights now.'

'How did *you* know about Rufus?'

'Well, I wasn't thinking straight and for some reason I thought that the note at the cottage might have been from you, so I read it. You know what it said, "Rufus, go straight to Terry's house. Everything will be fine. Liza".'

'What did you do then?'

'We went straight to the police. They had already heard from the Brownlea Police Station about Rufus of course, and they thought you'd planned something between you.'

'I s'pose it *was* a bit odd, both of us going missing together.'

'And you have no idea where he might be?'

'No, honest! Didn't you tell the police about Gran?'

139

'Yes, of course, but they still weren't convinced you hadn't arranged to meet him somewhere. It was only when I read this morning's paper I learned that Zebedee was still alive and on the Island, but I still didn't think that you would be there with him!'

Terry left the table. 'Let's have a look.'

His mother handed him the paper. 'Here, take it upstairs with you while you bath. Your father and the police inspector will be back any minute and they want a word with you.'

Terry sat on the edge of the bath while it filled, reading the paper. There were two photographs. One of himself with a gloomy expression. He was holding a picture of Zebedee and the large SOLD was showing on the agent's board in the background. The caption above it read 'PRIZE DONKEY'S HOME SOLD'. The other photograph was of Zebedee himself, grazing on the Island. 'TIME AND TIDE RUN OUT FOR HOMELESS ZEBEDEE' it stated. Terry was impressed. They must have gone straight from here and hired a boat to the Island. The report explained the temporary nature of his stay on the Island and how he had been led there by 'caring youngsters'. Terry wondered what Fiona would make of that! Or more to the point what Mr Fells would say. Luckily, Mr Fells wasn't mentioned by name, and the actual ownership of the donkey and the field was rather skated over.

He almost fell asleep in the warm bath, jerking awake when his mother called from downstairs that his father was back. He dressed hurriedly and went down to face the music. But his father, looking white and tired, just gave him a hug, and the police inspector was more interested in any clue Terry might give him to Rufus's whereabouts than telling him off about his own behaviour.

'You're *quite* sure, Terry? You don't know where he might be? Any idea at all?' he asked for the third time.

'Honestly, I don't. I'd tell you if I did. Only Rufus doesn't talk a lot and when he does it's usually about bottles.'

'Like the one he sold before he left?'

'That's right. He was mad keen on collecting them.'

'Yet he sold his best one?'

'That's because he wanted his mother back. I told you what he said to me that morning about his dad having a busted head and his mother being away all the time.'

The inspector sighed. 'Yes, all right lad. It all points one way. He wanted to get to the Peace Camp and he had the money for the fare. so where *is* he?'

He stood up to go and Terry's father walked to the front door to see him out. Terry heard him saying something about press and television cover. He felt cold, remembering his own lonely night on the Island. Where was Rufus sleeping? No one had set eyes on him since he'd got mad with Fay Donovan . . .

'Fay Donovan!' he yelled.

'What?' His mother stared at him, but Terry ran past her to the front door. 'Wait a minute!'

'Remembered something lad?' the inspector asked.

'That lady, the one from the camp who called with the news about their mother.'

'What about her? We've spoken to her, she's back in Brownlea with the others. She doesn't know anything.'

'She came in a van.' Terry began to feel rather foolish.

'That's right. A green Austin.'

'And she said she was going back. That she'd only come to deliver the news. But Rufus wasn't there when she said she was going to visit the family of the other lady that was arrested. S'pose Rufus thought she was going straight back? He might have hidden in the back of the van.'

The inspector looked interested. 'Good thinking. And this Fay Donovan went to where?'

'I don't know. She just said she was spending the night with them.'

'Never mind, we can soon find out. Well done, lad, at least it gives us some kind of lead.'

'Do let us know if there's any news,' Terry's mother said as he left.

His father had to hear the whole story then, and his mother managed to think up a whole new load of questions. When he had finished Terry gave a huge yawn. 'I think I'll go to bed. I didn't get much sleep last night.'

'Neither did we,' his father said, doing his best to sound annoyed. But Terry could see he was quite impressed about him rowing to the Island alone.

'You're lucky that man came along when he did,' his mother said, 'the Island is the last place we'd have thought of looking, knowing how you feel about water.'

'What's his name?' his father asked. 'I must go and thank him.'

'I don't know. *I* call him Captain Madcap. That's the name of his boat. He's really nice. He was going to take me to the Island on Saturday to fill up Zebedee's tank if the others didn't get back.'

142

'The things you've been up to! I can't get over it! Go on, off to bed,' his mother said as he gave another yawn.

He slept for four hours then his mother shook him awake. 'Fiona is on the phone, pretending to be the lady from Smith's! I told her to reverse the charges.' He stumbled downstairs, still half asleep.

'Terry? They've found him. It's been awful here with Ma and Liza both blaming themselves. The police picked him up a few miles from Bristol.'

'Is he all right?'

'Fine, apparently. They'll be bringing him here this evening.'

'Where had he been? What happened to him?'

'We don't know much yet. He *did* hide in the van and then got out when Fay went into the people's house in Aberystwyth. He thought he was at the Peace Camp.'

'What was he doing in Bristol then? That's miles away, isn't it?'

'Can't tell you much more yet. I'll write. It's murder trying to phone from this place, there's always a queue. This call must be costing your mother a fortune anyway. How's Zeb?'

'He's fine, but Fiona . . .'

'I'll write tonight. Can't stop. Oh, and Terry . . .'

'Yes?'

'I'm glad I met your Gran.' And she was gone.

He put the phone back. 'They've found him and he's okay,' he told his mother, who was waiting for news.

'Thank goodness for that. Where was he?'

'Outside Bristol.'

'He didn't get far in two days. Where had he been?'

'He went via Aberystwyth. He *did* hide in the van like I said. Fiona is going to write tonight and tell me the rest. They haven't actually seen Rufus yet.'

He wandered out into the hot sunshine. He wished there was somewhere he could write to Fiona himself or, better still, ring her. They only had a week left. It was Friday, and school started on Monday. Where could he find a field in a week? The lowest tides were the weekend after they started school. He went back into the house to ask his mother if it would be all right to use his fifty pounds to keep Zebedee somewhere, always providing they could find somewhere, but she was on the phone making arrangements about the funeral. He went back into the garden sobered by the thought.

For the rest of the day Terry drifted, unable to settle to anything. Even when he tried drawing the cat from down the lane, there wasn't the usual magic. After tea he went down to the harbour to see Captain Madcap.

'Well? Everything shipshape?' the captain greeted him.

'They weren't mad. They were too pleased to see me.'

'You're lucky.' He handed him two oars. 'There you are, it's not a bad match. I'll keep my eyes peeled for the one you lost. They sometimes get washed up.'

'How much do I owe you?'

'Borrow it for a bit till we see if yours turns up. If it doesn't we'll come to a fair price.'

'Thanks a lot.' Terry carried the oars back along the beach to the cottage and put them safely in the shed. He was longing to hear all the details about Rufus and to tell them about his own adventure.

144

All the way home he worried at the problem of Zebedee's future, but couldn't come up with any new ideas. It looked as if they were going to have to confess defeat to Mr Fells next week. If he had to pay for the oar that would knock a small hole in his money, and anyway, fifty pounds might sound a lot, but it would only buy them a few weeks' breathing space.

That night he tossed and turned, wishing Fiona would come home to share the problem again.

Good News

The next day, Saturday, was the last weekend before starting school. Gran's funeral was on Tuesday and he had told his mother that he wanted to be there. She had looked doubtful but hadn't argued.

The post brought an unusually large amount of mail. 'Is there one for me from Fiona?' he asked eagerly as his father went through the pile.

'They're all for you,' his father said, handing him the letters. 'Half a dozen!'

'Crimes!' Terry said. 'Who are they from?'

'Fan-mail?' his mother suggested. 'After your photo appeared n the paper?'

He recognised Fiona's spidery scrawl and put it aside. The others were all offers of homes for Zebedee! He read them one after the other, his face flushed with excitement. 'Look, here's another one! "Dear sir, I have a very large lawn which your donkey would be welcome to graze for the winter." That's hopeless of course, but it's nice of them to offer.'

'Let me see.' His mother read out a postcard written in a childish scrawl. ' "My shed would keep your donkey warm all winter and I would share my cornflakes."'

When Terry had sorted the six letters concerning Zebedee there were three practical possibilities. Two were on smallholdings quite a long way away, but the third was right in town. 'This is fantastic! Just wait till I tell Fiona. If only I could phone her! I'll go and check this one out this afternoon.'

He went out into the garden to read her letter last of all. It was hard to decipher, being written on a collection of torn open paper bags, and handwriting was not one of her talents, but finally he managed it.

Dear Terry, she wrote,

Cheesy grins all round now Ruf is safe. Ma's been to court and is out on bail (money by courtesy of Josh's pawned flute!). The date for the hearing hasn't been fixed, so I still don't know when we'll be coming home. Sorry about Zeb but there's nothing I can do. Still, it should be easier now that your Ma and Pa know ALL!

About Ruf. He's quite laid back about it all. He hid in Fay's van under some blankets. They drove for hours — Ruf thinking they were going back to Brownlea and Fay driving to Aberystwyth. (Which in case you don't know is in the opposite direction.) When they reached the house she got out and Ruf sneaked a look and just saw a street. He had no idea what the camp would look like so he climbed out, did a reccy, and found the sea! Well, even Ruf knows there's no sea in Brownlea, so he climbed back in.

He had food and drink in his haversack so he slept in the van all night, then next morning did another reccy and discovered it was Aberystwyth and realised he'd blown it!

Terry, searching for the next piece of paper bag, tried to imagine his own reaction given the same situation, and decided that at that point he would have called it a day. But Rufus hadn't.

147

He went back, meaning to get in the van again, but it was gone. Fay had got up early and left, leaving Rufus stranded.

He was a bit hazy about how far Aberystwyth was from Brownlea so he went to the railway station and asked. When the man told him he would have to change trains three times and cough up nearly fifteen quid, he decided to buy a map and start to walk! But in a café he got talking to two boys who offered him a lift as far as Cheltenham. It seemed like a good offer, but when they stopped at one of the Services for petrol the tank was locked and they didn't have the key. Rufus was already suspicious. (He thought they might have pinched the car to go joy-riding, they were lousy drivers, he said) so he hid in a loo till they were gone. Then he walked and hitched for miles as far as Chepstow.

Then he went to buy something to eat, and discovered they'd pinched his money, so he spent the rest of the night in the Services and the next day he was picked up on a B-road outside Bristol after walking over the Severn Bridge. I think he'd just about had enough by then, so he came quietly! (The car was found later smashed up and the two boys were injured, and they admitted taking his money.)

Must dash and post this so can't write any more. Hope to see you before DR Day (Donkey Retrieving Day). Keep Home Hunting. Your Partner In Crime. Fiona.

Terry folded the letter slowly, impressed by Rufus's determination. Remembering his own night on the

Island he knew he would have legged it to the nearest police station a lot sooner than that. He went into the house and gave his mother a censored version of the story.

'Okay if I go and look at this paddock of Mr Murphy's?'

'Yes, of course, but hadn't you better tell Mr Fells about it first? After all, Zebedee *is* still his donkey.'

'I suppose so.' He went to the phone reluctantly. Zeb felt like *his* donkey. He heaved a sigh of relief when no one answered. Knowing Rufus was safe left his mind free to worry about Zeb.

Walking down the hill towards town, he faced the fact that if Fiona didn't get back before next week-end then shifting the donkey would be left to him. Remembering how Zebedee stopped for no reason on the way out and just stood, he felt all his misgivings about the sea returning. Zebedee was enjoying life on the Island. There was a fair chance that he wouldn't want to leave and Terry didn't feel over-confident about persuading him.

An hour later he was back home. 'It's perfect Mum. Just what we've been praying for, and there it was, right in town, just as if it was waiting for him. And Mr Murphy is great, he says he'll look after him when we can't get there.'

He tried Mr Fells' number again, this time hoping someone *was* in to share the good news, but there was still no reply.

Terry spent the rest of the afternoon answering the other letters, thanking them but explaining that Zebedee was fixed. He wished he could write to Fiona but had no address. If only she would phone again! Before sealing the envelopes he sorted out some of his Zebedee sketches and enclosed one with each reply.

'That's a good idea Terry,' his father said. 'They may be worth a fortune one day.' Which made Terry feel good.

End of the Holiday

On Monday school restarted. Terry enjoyed a mild notoriety as a result of the newspaper article. Boys who normally didn't bother with him asked him about taking the donkey to the Island, and after break Old Careworn sent for him.

'Well,' he said. 'Hiding your light under a bushel?' Terry shifted awkwardly, unable to explain why his classwork was so poor, restricted by the limitations the Art teacher put on him.

Fiona was still away. Every morning he looked hopefully down on the deserted cottage as he walked to school, but no bright splash of colour told him the Daisy-bus was back in its usual place.

On Tuesday he had a day off to attend Gran's funeral. Dressed uncomfortably in a new grey suit, he stood next to his mother and father, thinking that none of this had anything to do with Gran. Not as he remembered her.

There weren't many people in church. If Fiona and her family had been home would they have come, he wondered? Gran was old and had outlived a lot of her friends.

He tried to join in the singing, feeling he was letting her down but his throat was thick, and his tongue too big for his mouth. Instead he conjured up a picture of her in her room at home, feeding the tame robin at the window. A picture so vivid that he wanted to shout suddenly that it was all a mistake and they needn't go on with the service.

Then suddenly it was over and they were driving to the cemetery and he slipped his arm through his mother's to comfort her because she was crying.

She looked down at him surprised, and gave him a watery smile. He was relieved when he was able to take off the awful clothes and escape down the harbour where he went to see Captain Madcap.

'If you can take me to the Island next Saturday morning at eight o'clock I'll have plenty of time to wait for the tide to drop and then walk Zebedee back.'

'You've found a place for him then?'

'A super place, and no charge! I'll pay you for the boat-trip, and that oar,' he added.

The captain puffed his pipe thoughtfully. 'Tell you what lad, what about me getting a spot of publicity out of this?'

'How d'you mean?'

'You know the kind of thing. A photo of Zebedee for my board.' He nodded to his blackboard advertising trips. ' "Refugee Donkey Returns to Mainland". "Owner Charters Madcap for Island Rescue". Fetch me in a fortune next season that will. The public love a spot of Animal Crackers.'

'I don't mind, but he's not really *my* donkey. Mr Fells is his real owner,' Terry said.

'We'll worry about that when the time comes. In the meantime I'll arrange to take some pictures. I'm a bit of a dab hand at photography. Is it a deal?'

The rest of the week passed slowly. On Thursday a postcard arrived from Fiona. It said, 'Hearing fixed. Hope to be back in time for DR Day. Liza got job.

Fiona.' Terry looked at the date stamp. It had been posted three days before.

And still they hadn't come back. He rang the Fells' house a few more times without success and then on Friday evening there was a call for him from Mrs Fells. 'Terry? I'm ringing from Belgium.

'Crimes!'

'I thought we'd be back but we've been delayed. Business. Now, about Zebedee . . .'

'It's all right. I've found him a home. It's perfect.'

'Oh good. I'm so pleased and relieved. Can you manage, you and Fiona?'

'Yes, of course.' He didn't see any point in telling her that Fiona was away.

'Right then, good luck!' The connection was cut. He replaced the receiver slowly. So it was all up to him. He didn't think his parents had ever registered the dates of the tides and the importance of getting Zebedee back this weekend, and he saw no point in reminding them.

On Saturday he woke early and walked over to the harbour, shouldering the knapsack that he had packed with lunch and carrots and a halter the night before.

'Right, jump aboard!' Captain Madcap was ready and waiting. As he started the engine and the little craft nosed its way between the other boats and out towards the harbour entrance, Terry no longer dreaded the boat trips. Somewhere along the way, his fear of the sea had receded. He certainly respected it, and would prefer to be *on* it rather than *in* it, but it was as familiar as an old friend. Perhaps he would have a serious bash at learning to swim in school this winter.

Zebedee came trotting to meet them as they landed.

Terry made a fuss of him, pulling the long ears. 'Time to go home boy. The holidays are over.' He fed him a carrot.

'Right, we'll have one of you both standing in front of the boat,' the captain called, producing his camera, 'I want to make sure the name of the boat is in it.'

Terry grinned. 'I'd forgotten all about the pictures.'

'Got it. That should be a good one. I'll be watching you and waiting at the other end to get a few more.' He started the engine and chugged away, the swell pushing up the waves around Terry's feet.

Terry climbed the slope with Zebedee following, glad that it was a warm, dry morning. He sat on the cropped turf and waited for the level of water to drop, sharing his sandwiches with Zebedee and thinking of all that had happened since they'd brought him here.

He thought about Fiona, and what might be happening in Brownlea. Gran and the funeral. The newspaper article and the Art competition that had led to him finding the paddock.

At last the tide had dropped enough to expose the shining wet rocks and seaweed of the causeway. Terry got to his feet and took the rope halter from his knapsack and slipped it over the donkey's head. Then he threw the remains of his breakfast to the gulls and led him towards the path.

It was much easier in daylight and he had the comforting knowledge that Captain Madcap was waiting at the other end if anything should go wrong. But Zebedee stepped out confidently, keeping close to Terry and avoiding the rock pools. Fifteen minutes later they were on firm sand.

As his front hooves touched the wet sand, Zebedee

turned and, looking back, gave his raucous bray. Terry, raising his eyes from his intense concentration of the uneven track, yelled himself. 'Fiona!'

She was racing across the beach, red hair flying. 'Terry! You did it! On your own!'

'Right, one either side! Hold it!' The captain was clicking away again.

'We rushed to get back. I didn't know till last night, so I couldn't ring. Where's Mr Fells? Where are you taking him?' She was bubbling with questions.

Terry introduced her to the captain and explained what a help he'd been. Then they waved him goodbye and led Zebedee up the beach, talking non-stop. Terry could feel his face split in one big grin he was so pleased to see her.

Then he saw Rufus, standing by a small neat woman with dark braided hair. She looked no taller than Fiona. He realised it was their mother and felt suddenly shy. He remembered the nightmare figure of his dreams on the Island and felt embarrassed, as if she might know about them. Then she and Rufus came to meet them and she said, 'So this is Terry who loved his Gran and rescued Zebedee.' And he didn't feel shy any more.

'Hi Rufus,' he said. 'Glad you made it.'

'Hi Terry. Glad *you* made it.'

They all laughed. 'Where's Liza and the others?' Terry asked. 'And how did the . . .' He hesitated, not knowing what word to use. Trial? Hearing? Court case?

Their mother helped him out. 'I was fined twenty pounds for disturbing the peace. Rather ironic for a peace lady, isn't it?' She laughed and with it Terry realised why Rufus wanted so much for her to come back.

'Liza and Josh are both in London,' Fiona said. 'Liza's started her new job and Josh . . .'

'Brother Josh is interviewing for Music colleges.' Larry had come out of the cottage. 'Kettle's on. Anyone for a cuppa?'

They left Zebedee grazing on the lawn and went into the cottage. To Terry it was like coming home. 'I didn't know Josh wanted to go to a Music college,' he said.

'Neither did anyone else. We all assumed he wanted Cambridge like me. That'll teach me to count my chickens,' Larry said ruefully.

'I didn't think you needed to go to Cambridge University to learn to count chickens,' Rufus seemed chattier now his mother was home.

'Quiet pest, you're more than half responsible,' Larry said, laughing with the others.

'How d'you make that out?' Fiona said.

'Because Josh said if young Rufus had the bottle to go after what *he* wanted, then he should too. He'd been going off the idea of being a mathematician all summer but hadn't had the guts to admit it, even to himself.'

'Dad's coming home soon as well.' Rufus said, 'for a couple of months.'

'He'll be able to get Josh's flute out of the hock-shop. That's how we paid for the petrol to go to Brownlea and Ma's bail,' Fiona said.

Terry told them all about his night on the Island. He admitted taking the boat and losing the oar. The more he saw of their mother the more he liked her. She was like Gran. She really listened and only asked the sort of questions that made sense.

Larry only said, 'Your rowing must have come on

156

a treat. P'raps Josh is right. He ought to be a teacher. Perhaps he'll compose Music *and* teach. It wouldn't be a bad life.'

'But you still haven't told us *where* we're taking him,' Fiona said when he reached the part about the letters offering homes.

'Wait and see,' he said, irritatingly, and refused to say more.

They set off, walking through the busy Saturday streets in town and into the suburbs where the streets were wider and the houses more spaced out, Zebedee following obediently.

When they reached the town cemetery, Terry stopped. 'This is where Gran is buried,' he said and walked through the gates.

'Is it? Are we going to visit her now? Should we take Zebedee in?' she asked, looking puzzled.

Terry didn't answer. He gave her the rope and walked up to a red brick house in the corner and knocked on the door. A small cheery-looking man opened it. 'Ah, there we are then. And this is the famous creature himself.' He had a soft Irish brogue.

'Hello, Mr Murphy. This is Fiona and this is Zebedee.'

'Bring yourselves round here then and we'll see what Molly makes of him.'

'Is Molly his wife?' Fiona whispered as he led them along a path to the back of the house. Terry shook his head.

The small man opened a wooden gate at the end of the garden and they were in a grassy paddock surrounded by trees. There was a stone shelter in one corner.

'Come on Molly, me beauty, and meet your new companion,' he called. 'For it's that lonely the poor little creature's been since Moloney took off for the Great Pastures in the Sky.' He winked at them.

A pretty brown and white nanny goat came prancing across the grass and butted the man playfully. 'Moloney was an old beach pony I had till last month when he died of old age and nothing more lethal,' said the man, who seemed to find the subject a bit of a joke. Perhaps, Terry thought, it was being a caretaker and living in the middle of a cemetery.

The little nanny sniffed at Zebedee's nose. 'Bedam, she likes him!' he yelled. 'She had that very same expression when she met Moloney.'

'But will Zebedee like *her*?' Fiona asked, patting the pretty little creature. 'Mrs Fells said he's a loner.'

'We'll not have long to wait and see. Lead him out lad and let's see what they're about.'

Terry led Zebedee around the field and the little nanny goat followed. 'Right, slip the rope,' Mr Murphy called and Terry did so. Zebedee set off to explore his new home with Molly following closely.

'I don't see any trouble there but I'll watch them just in case, never you worry. I've a further paddock beyond so I can separate them if needs be.'

'Thank you ever so much. We were getting desperate,' Terry said.

'And don't forget my picture now. It'll make a grand gift for the wife's birthday next month.'

'No, I won't. I'll start sketching tomorrow. Molly *and* Zeb. I've promised one for Mrs Fells as well. He'll be getting famous, hung on so many walls.'

They stood watching the two animals settle to graze, staying close. Then they walked homewards through the cemetery.

It was good having Fiona back. He remembered the

flat grey day when he'd first met her on the beach at the very start of the summer holidays.

'When you think of all the things that have gone on this holiday!' she said, echoing his thoughts, as she so often did.

They walked on, making plans, stopping briefly by Gran's grave. As Terry said, it was nice to think of Gran close by. She had always loved Zebedee.

If you liked this book then why not
look out for other Kelpies. There are
more than fifty titles to choose from
and they are available from all good bookshops.

For a free Kelpie badge, catalogue and
any other information, please send
a stamped addressed envelope to:
Margaret Ritchie (K.C.B.)
Canongate Publishing Ltd.,
16 Frederick Street, Edinburgh EH2 2HB